STRANGERS
AT THE PORT

Also by Lauren Aimee Curtis

Dolores

STRANGERS
AT THE PORT

LAUREN AIMEE CURTIS

W&N
WEIDENFELD & NICOLSON

First published in Great Britain in 2023 by Weidenfeld & Nicolson,
an imprint of The Orion Publishing Group Ltd
Carmelite House, 50 Victoria Embankment
London EC4Y 0DZ

An Hachette UK Company

1 3 5 7 9 10 8 6 4 2

This project has been assisted by the Australian Government through the
Australia Council, its arts funding and advisory body.

The author wishes to thank the Australia Council and The Society of Authors.

A CIP catalogue record for this book is
available from the British Library.

ISBN (Hardback) 978 1 3996 0816 9
ISBN (Export Trade Paperback) 978 1 3996 0817 6
ISBN (eBook) 978 1 3996 0819 0
ISBN (Audio) 978 1 3996 0820 6

Typeset by Input Data Services, Bridgwater, Somerset

Printed in Great Britain by Clays Ltd, Elcograf S.p.A.

www.weidenfeldandnicolson.co.uk
www.orionbooks.co.uk

My suffering is only noble when I put it into words.

Fernando Pessoa
The Book of Disquiet

PART ONE

GIULIA

1

Of all the islands in the archipelago, ours was the greenest and ours was the richest. Our volcanoes lay dormant. Our soil was fertile. Our wine was famous – desired for its sweetness. It surprised the tongue and warmed the belly.

Our wine was requested by kings and queens. Our wine was guzzled at royal banquets. Even the British army, stationed at Messina, demanded our wine – got drunk on our wine – on their idle afternoons waiting for Napoleon.

Long before this, our island emerged from the Tyrrhenian Sea. Our island began with volcanic eruptions. It had been home to the Greeks, the Carthaginians, the Romans, the Arabs, the Normans, and who knows who else by the time we arrived.

Pirates ravaged our island. Shepherds kept their flocks on our empty hills. Monks built shrines while they waited out exile. Since the very beginning, it seems, people came to our island, settled, then fled.

2

I knew no history. I had little concept of time beyond the harvest seasons, the changing weather. When I stood on the fishing dock as a child and looked out at the other islands in the archipelago, I was not thinking of battleships or explorers or sea monsters from mythologies. I was not thinking about what came before or what lay beyond.

What can I tell you about my young life on the island? It is shrouded in the mystery of childhood itself. I try to picture myself, age ten, for that is the time when the 'trouble' – as you call it – began. But I don't have an image of this girl. I can't see her from the outside. There are no photographs. Besides, I don't trust them.

I could tell you that my only true friend on the island, apart from my older sister, Giovanna, was a donkey with weepy eyes and long lashes. A white patch of fur on his belly I took pleasure in scratching. A rusted bell hung around his neck. He had a bung leg. We called him Shuffles. *What is the significance of this donkey?* I imagine you asking. Nothing, nothing. Except to say that when he was deemed useless we cared for him. Fed him apples. Tied scarves around his head. A big bow between the ears. I remember thinking I would marry him when the time came. I remember thinking this as if it were the most normal thought in the world.

Do you see what I am trying to say? Our world was very small. When I was ten and Giovanna was twelve, we had never left our island, not even for the others in the archipelago. We knew the islands surrounding us not by their proper names but by what they resembled: a turtle, a dog lying down, a mountain, a jagged crown. Those islands were black or grey or brown depending on the position of the sun. Ours was emerald green.

Every morning, Giovanna and I went down to the fishing dock to watch the water. We could tell if rain was coming by where the clouds hung in the sky (this, we learnt from the fishermen). From May to September, it hardly rained at all. The cisterns on our roofs went dry, and the smell of dead fish – thick in the summer

– wafted through the circular hole above the door of our bungalow, even when our mother stuffed it with rags.

Although we lived at the bottom of the island in a small fishing village, we still felt we were better than the people who lived on the opposite side of the island by the port. The port people were ignoble, Mother told us, because they cavorted with the sailors, and they were not ashamed to live near the rubbish heap. Besides, the port was ugly. The port was not a well-regarded place. Even where we lived – in the damp, narrow alleyways above the fishing dock – had more prestige than the port! Between the two villages was a large valley with vineyards planted all over the slopes. Two mountains – our two sleeping volcanoes – stood on either side. On our island, the higher you lived, the richer you were. Still, our little village was respected. In the evenings, everyone gathered in our square. Most nights, we saw amber specks fizzling against the black sky coming from the volcano on the island opposite. Little spurts of lava that shot up rhythmically. A constant, hazy glow. We knew those amber specks meant danger for the people on that island, but we were on the green island, and so we cared little.

You must understand: from birth we had been told

that our island was rich in resources. We had no need to worry – the shipmaster would take care of us all.

He was the only person who routinely left and returned. Left not just for the other islands in the archipelago, but for unknowable places beyond. He brought back gifts. He had a gold cane with a goose-head handle, and he took it with him on his walks around the square. The way that he moved – slowly, gracefully – signalled his difference to the rest of us. He did not stumble. He rarely yelled. If I close my eyes, I can see him standing at the balustrade at the edge of our square looking out at the sea below. His long beard is neatly combed and turning grey at the tips. His lips are hidden underneath his thick moustache. There he is walking past the baker's shop and raising his cane. Now the baker's daughter is running out.

He was a king to us. A god. At the very least, our protector. Really, he was a trader in exports who commandeered an impressive fleet.

All of us in the village, whenever we saw him, would make a little gesture as he passed us. Mother bowed her head, so Giovanna and I did the same. The fishermen only ever spoke to him with eyes averted and their hands clasped firmly behind their backs. The older widows fussed over him. Often, they tried to kiss his hand. Once, the baker's son saluted him, and we – all of us in the square – had to wait until the shipmaster was out of sight to let out our laughter. Our bellies sore from holding it in. It was the baker's daughter, though, who embarrassed us most with her confusing gestures. Whenever she held out the bread, she squatted before him – an awkward curtsey – and we had to look away.

There was another embarrassing woman in our village. A widow, like Mother, who went about in an evening gown that was torn and yellowing. This woman refused to wear black. She had no tact, Mother told us, because she wore her hair in the manner of the ship-master's wife. Uncovered, that is, and twirled into two shapes that looked like snail shells, pinned at the nape of her neck. She lived alone, and although she tried to hide it, she spent her nights in the grotto near the port where the other drunks met. To get there, you had to wait until the tide was low and climb along the rocks. People talked about a secret path, a way to get there from the lighthouse above, but none of us ever found it.

There was a rumour about the woman leaving the grotto one night and throwing herself into the sea. Apparently, she had to be fished out. When she came to, she told the rest of the drunks that she had merely wanted to wash her dress. She clambered over the rocks and left the wet gown on the roof of her bungalow to dry. We knew this, because the baker had seen it there.

This woman – still so large in my mind – does not appear in your book, Professor. I woke up this morning with the thought that I could write to you. That I could tell you some of the things you missed.

According to your version of events, an insect pest arrived on our island hidden in some bits of wood and destroyed all of our vines. Excuse me for saying, but you seem obsessed with the aphid! Forty pages on its breeding cycle, its microscopic body, its way of burying itself into the roots – imperceptible to our eyes. When you explain its method of sucking the life from our vines, I detect a certain relish. You appear like a young, excitable boy at a science fair presenting his hypothesis.

There is no mention of the shipmaster in your book, nothing about our village. There is nothing about the men who arrived on our island in the spring before the vines began to die. You must not realise what an event it was. We did not know they were coming. No one had told us about the new law. We were not expecting a ship of prisoners in the archipelago. Professor, when I was a child, I did not know what a prison was.

3

That spring, when the men arrived, I was ten years old, wearing a dress made of muslin and a red woollen cloak, holding on to Mother's hand as we walked down the hill to the market by the port. We saw an unfamiliar ship in the distance – saw the white trail it left in the water as it approached our island. By the time we reached the market, the ship had docked. The gangplank dropped and the men came walking out. I counted twelve. Everyone at the market stopped to watch. We did not know they were prisoners. We only saw a group of strangers. They were both young and old, with beards roughly clipped, wearing grey tunics. Some of them were paler, but most had our hue – that is, olive-skinned, as they say today, though I don't understand what an olive has to do with it. One of the men stood out for his honey-coloured hair, the tufts on his cheeks that glinted in the sun, but the rest looked similar to the men on our island. Later, Mother said that they looked nothing like our men.

In her memory of their arrival, it was always raining. But the sun was out, I remember – the first feeling of warmth on the skin after a long winter, though the wind was cold and brisk. The men stood on the dock with their tunics fluttering and their faces tilted towards the sun. Two guards – wearing jackets with bright buckles and large black hats – emerged from the belly of the ship. They jostled the men into the back of the shipmaster's largest carriage. The mules were whipped. The carriage travelled in the direction of Mount Fern, and we followed it. Half our village were trailing behind, looking up at the men while they stared back at us. One of them even blew us kisses! I saw his head bobbing above the crowd.

When we reached the valley, the carriage stopped outside the shipmaster's house. We kept our distance and hid behind the trees. We did not talk to each other for fear that the shipmaster would hear us. He was already waiting outside his gates when we arrived. He spoke to the guards and then motioned for his driver to continue up the mountain. This time we were unable to follow. The shipmaster was looking out at the trees where we were hiding. He held his gaze. Little ripples. My skin felt prickly from his stare. One by one, we came out from our hiding spots and walked silently back to the market.

That evening, everyone was in the square pretending to look busy. Really, we were waiting for the shipmaster. Waiting for him, on his evening walk, to tell us who these men were and what they were doing on our island.

Giovanna was with me and Mother, and she was jealous. She had not been at the port when the men arrived. We were standing near the path that led up to the forest, waiting for the shipmaster to appear among the trees. Meanwhile, the baker's daughter was doing laps around the square, talking to anyone who would listen to her about the men. She was telling us she did not need any more amorous advances; the shipmaster's sons were enough to deal with.

An hour passed. The sky and the sea turned orange, then pink, a reddish purple. Wind came hurtling around the cliffs. We were silent. Listening for footsteps when all we could hear were cicadas, the wind whis-tling, the rocks being dragged into the sea on the beach below. Mother went inside the church with the others to pray, but the wooden doors flew open while they were kneeling, extinguishing their lit candles. A bad omen, we thought.

Night came. It was cold and dark, and no one had thought to bring lanterns. We were not expecting to be out for so long. At the entrance to the church, our priest was sweeping sand out of the doorway. He was telling us it was time to go home. He went inside to ring the bells. We heard them chime nine times.

The shipmaster never came to the square that night, and rarely did he miss his evening walk. His absence was not only unusual; it felt threatening. As you can imagine, Professor, it only inflamed our curiosity about the men.

4

As far back as I could remember, there had been no new inhabitants on our island. No visitors, apart from the sailors, who only stayed a day or so, and even then, we rarely saw them. They kept to the port side and spent their nights in the grotto. Only once had I seen a sailor close up. I was at the market with Mother and wandered off. The tide was low. I saw a body splayed out over the rocks – his back arched. His face was bloated and his pale tongue was sticking out. He had drowned. I know that now. At the time, Mother told me he was sleeping.

We knew that the men were staying on our island, but we did not know why. In those first days, their presence was not properly explained. They were being kept on Mount Fern, sleeping among ruins that none of us would go near because a child had died there, and it was thought to be a place that brought bad luck. We heard they were working in the shipmaster's fields on the port side. But the baker's wife said she had seen them walking through the forest that bordered on our square. At this, she was indignant.

About a week after they arrived, Giovanna and I came upon the men bathing in an inlet at the edge of our village. They looked so nervous as they waded into the waist-deep water, holding their privates as they crouched down to splash their armpits, faces and backs. Not one of them put their head underneath. We thought perhaps they could not swim. We were lying on our bellies on the cliff above, watching them, loose rocks scattered around us. Without saying a word, Giovanna picked one up and threw it off the edge. It broke the water below and the men looked up. Days later, we returned at the hour we knew they would be bathing, both of us gathering rocks along the way.

Do I feel some shame in writing this? Yes. But we were frightened of them. Unsettled by what the adults around us said. If we threw rocks at them, it was because we feared them. But we also found their presence oddly thrilling. The other islands in the archipelago had their active volcanoes; now we had the men.

We overheard the women in our village warning

Mother not to walk alone at night. They told her to listen for the trumpet each evening, telling the men to return to Mount Fern, where they would be counted by one of the shipmaster's sons.

Have I mentioned his sons? He had nine. Some of them were smaller than us, but the older ones carried rifles. It was not unusual to come across them in the square, racing one another around the benches or straddling the mermaid statue that stood near the church. Sometimes we heard shots echoing through the forest when they were hunting rabbits in the valley above. They dressed differently from the sons of the fishermen in our village – wearing long trousers that covered their ankles and shirts made from fine linen. Whenever the shipmaster was away from our island, they would knock on the drunk widow's window at all hours, singing songs about taking an ugly wife or a woman with a bosom so big that she had to walk with a stick. As a group, they were intimidating. There were so many of them! This was, according to Mother, the real reason why the shipmaster's wife rarely left her house. *Nine sons would break any woman,* is what Mother often said. The youngest was five and had an especially large head. Mother said it would have been his ears that hurt the shipmaster's wife the most, pointy as they were, like wings.

5

Our mother slept with a grimace – her mouth folded downwards – and sometimes a word, seemingly foreign, would shoot out of her mouth, so that Giovanna and I had to rub her back to wake her. The three of us shared one bed. Our father died when I was young, and as a child I had trouble picturing him. He always ended up looking a little bit like the shipmaster, only wearing the calico pants and red cloak of a fisherman. This secret image – treasure of all treasures – was ruined by my sister. *You wouldn't have any memories of him*, is what Giovanna said. But I did have memories! Of hairy hands filling a pipe with tobacco, the smell of smoke and brine on his wiry beard, a voice – soft and low – singing to us in the early evening. *None of that is real*, Giovanna would tell me, smiling triumphantly.

All my life, my sister never let me forget that she had

been a second mother to me. I was late to walk and talk. According to Giovanna, I used to point to my open mouth and she would know to feed me. It was her, and not Mother – Giovanna said – who taught me how to speak. *Mother always slept,* Giovanna would say. *I was the one who wrapped blankets around you!*

I was a docile child. Fearful. Obedient. All the things my sister was not.

We lived off the pity of our neighbours, who gave us fish, and the shipmaster, who was our true benefactor. Every week, one of his sons would appear at our door holding a pot of something warm from their cook or a few coins. Mother would take the coins and put them in the leather pouch she wore tied around her neck, while Giovanna and I watched from the bed.

But that spring, the sons stopped visiting. It happened abruptly. The shipmaster no longer took his evening walks in our square and his sons no longer knocked on our door. Mother said the shipmaster must be avoiding any questions we had about the men. She took herself to bed. Mother could sleep for hours if she wanted. Nobody could sleep like Mother. She told us that she knew how to sleep standing up. She had taught herself when she used to wake early and wait on the dock with the other wives for the fishermen to return.

6

Before the arrival of the men, our lives had always followed a steady rhythm. Our fields were ploughed in October and sown in November, then came the long sleep of winter. In spring, wildflowers – of the kind I have not seen since I left – would shoot up all over the island. We picked mulberries in May, figs from the end of June, plums in July, almonds in August. But the most important harvest – as you well know, Professor – was the grape harvest in the middle of September.

We were counting the days. It was only May. We thought the men might leave after the harvest. Although we were becoming used to the sound of the trumpet each evening telling the men to return from the shipmaster's fields, we would sometimes remember, quite suddenly, that there were strange men sleeping above us on our mountain. It was unnerving, to say the least.

One morning, we woke to find our mother in a cleaning frenzy. At first, she went about washing the walls, rubbing the windows with a bit of damp cloth, sweeping the floor and chasing the lizards out with her broom. Then she came after us – scrubbing our feet with pumice, cleaning out our eyes and ears with her wet fingers. She took a basket full of garments down to the stream where the fishermen's wives went to wash. We often heard them singing. Their songs were about their chores, the dangers of the sea, bad husbands, death. When Mother returned, she forced us into our dresses – now stiff and itchy – and swatted our hands when we went to scratch.

She stood in front of the mirror, combing her long hair and fixing it underneath her black kerchief. She dressed herself carefully, picking the blouse she wore on religious occasions and asking us for help with the tiny buttons at the back. At the door, right before we were about to leave, she tied a too-small bonnet around my head, one that I had not worn – Giovanna said – since I was baby. We began the long walk to the shipmaster's house.

He lived in the valley below Mount Fern. His house was the highest on our island. To get there, we had to cross the square and continue up through the forest where the ascent was steep. Mother kept stopping to catch her breath. By the time we got to the top, she was tugging at her neck where her blouse was tightly buttoned.

We walked through the valley, which was covered in vineyards. Rows and rows of the shipmaster's vines with green leaves that pointed outwards, the shape of rugged stars. At that time of year, the grapes were just tiny green berries, not nearly swollen enough to pick.

Below Mount Fern was the shipmaster's large house with the dark green shutters and the wide terrace that wrapped around it. There was a long driveway for his carriages flanked by large oaks and thin, spindly palms and pylons with marbled busts. Who were these men in marble form? we asked our mother, but she had no response. Until that day, Giovanna and I had never been beyond the front gates of the shipmaster's house.

Mother led us to a door at the back. It was the entrance to the kitchen. She knocked quickly and the shipmaster's housemaid appeared. She was hard of hearing. Mother had to bend down to speak while the housemaid loosened her kerchief and stuck out her ear. We followed her through the kitchen, down dark corridors, until she ushered us into a room, opened the thick curtains and told us to wait.

It was a parlour room, a place just for waiting. It felt like a palace. The walls were covered with paintings: portraits of the shipmaster's father, his father's father, his uncle, his father's uncle, his uncle's grandfather, and so on, in opulent gold frames. All of the men in his family had the same thick eyebrows and thin lips. The same small dark eyes. Only their beards were different – one completely white, another black and bushy, another trimmed into a triangular shape. They were frowning at us from above.

Other objects in the room beckoned. The plush green chairs arranged by the window were enticing. They looked like fluffy clouds. Tapestries hung from the walls, and patterned carpets covered the tiled floor. There were vases and woven baskets and a glass cabinet displaying models of the shipmaster's fleet. He commandeered sixty ships. Nine of them sailed to and from our island. Giovanna walked up to the cabinet and pressed her palms against the glass. She ran her fingers over the hardened paint of those portraits while Mother stood silently in the middle of the room, still tugging at her blouse where it buttoned at the neck. The housemaid returned. She stuck her head through the crack in the door and motioned for Mother – and Mother only – to follow her.

Then we were alone in the room, and it felt both grand and frightening. Giovanna and I collapsed on the green chairs. We played a game. Giovanna pretended to be the lady of the house while I was the housemaid. I bent down and nursed her sore feet. I rubbed her legs. *Hunch your shoulders!* she commanded, and I did. I was always the submissive one in our imagined scenes. I felt like a baby in my bonnet, and she told me I looked like one when I asked to switch roles. Then she stuck her fingers inside my nostrils. When I yelled, she put her sweaty hand over my mouth. A noise interrupted us. We heard an accordion manoeuvring over the shape of a melody, stopping and then starting once more. Giovanna went to the door to follow the sound. She disappeared into the dark corridor. Without her, I felt the men in the portraits looking at me differently. I could not bring myself to meet their eyes. I went to the window and looked outside, saw the shipmaster's sons walking through the vineyards. I counted to twenty, and then ran out into the corridor, opening doors, following the sound of the accordion, looking for my sister.

Had I been in a different state of mind, I might have taken pleasure in what I found in those other rooms: bronze busts, theatrical masks, painted landscapes, sculptures made from blown glass, velvet curtains with golden tassels, wooden chests with ornate carvings and, in one room, a large, gilded cage with a stuffed foreign bird – its feathers brightly coloured.

I came upon the two of them sitting together on a chaise. Giovanna was examining the accordion as the shipmaster's wife explained about the buttons. In my memory, that room is a violent shade of pink. I can still recall the way they both looked up. How the shipmaster's wife craned her long neck as she called out to the housemaid, her voice unexpectedly raspy.

On the way home, Mother's eyes were red. She was walking quickly through the forest, stopping to turn and scold us. *Who told you to go in there?* she was saying, but she was also asking questions. *What did she say to you? And her face? Were her cheeks red? Are her eyes like mine?* At this, she opened her eyes wide using her thumbs and fingers, so that she looked like an owl. Mother could get excitable like this sometimes.

I will fish, she was saying to herself as she marched towards the square. *I will fish*. But Mother did not know how to fish. She only knew how to gut them.

Days later, she returned to the shipmaster's house alone. When she came back, she told us that she would be starting work at the pumice quarry.

7

She cut a sharp figure standing against the white pumice cliffs in her black dress – Mother, who longed to wear her colours once more, and who liked to remind us that she was the youngest of all the widows on the island. In her trunk, she had a collection of silk scarves with patterned flowers and geometrical shapes – gifts from the shipmaster. Inside our bungalow with the door closed, she would experiment with different ways of tying them around her head and neck. There were certain things, Mother told us, that she could do at home, but not outside and certainly not in the square. At the time, I attributed the secrecy of Mother's ritual to the scarves themselves holding some kind of unspeakable power. I was frightened of those colourful scarves, Professor, and avoided the trunk she kept them in, which seemed to pulsate when I was in the room alone with it for too long.

Spring ended, summer came, and Mother got up early in the morning to wash her face at the basin by the light of the paraffin lamp. She plaited her long hair and pinned it underneath her kerchief, put on her big straw hat. When she returned in the late afternoons, she was always covered in flecks of fine white pumice. We found it in the crevasses of her skin, underneath her fingernails, inside her nostrils, on her eyelashes. She said she could feel it stuck inside her throat, no matter how much liquid she drank.

The pumice quarry was the place Giovanna and I used to go to during the winter months when we wanted to feel warm. On sunny days, the heat from the rock was like a flame licking our backs. It was the place we went when we were craving fatherly attention. We had known the quarry workers our whole lives, though most of them lived by the port. They liked it when we visited them, twirling in our dresses. We liked the high-pitched sound of their axes against the rock. Liked running our hands over the porous surface of the pumice and peering down into the mines, which were dark and damp and had an otherworldly smell.

Now, when Giovanna and I went to the quarry, it was

to visit Mother. We made a game of it. The game was this: the sad, young widow goes to work. Children are perverse, Professor. Surely you know this? We would dress in Mother's clothes, using a scarf to belt her dresses around our small waists, and cover our heads with black veils from her trunk. Then we would walk along the shore to the quarry pretending to sob. We liked the dramatic feeling it gave us. The adultness of it all. Most of all, we liked seeing the shadows of our bodies against those sun-drenched cliffs, which felt like a stage in front of the quarry workers. Those big white curtains!

In the beginning, Mother was bemused, or else she ignored us. She was easy to spot from a distance – the only widow sitting at the sorting table in her black dress surrounded by the other women in white. Their hands moved quickly over the mountainous pile in front them, feeling around for the right-size rock before tossing it in the appropriate sack. Those sacks, piled around them like a fortress, were later carried to small boats and rowed to the port. There, the quarry workers would form a line leading up to the ship. They would toss the sacks to one another, singing as they did so to keep their movements in perfect unison.

On certain days of the year, there would be a buzz in the air, everything jovial, everyone at the port on their best behaviour, and this meant the shipmaster himself was leaving. He would arrive before sunset, for that is when he liked to set out, in his best suit and sailing hat, his purple silk scarf tied at the neck. The horn would sound. Black smoke would emerge from the smokestack. He would stand on deck as the ship departed from our island, and we – those of us who came to watch – would wave to him as he raised his cane, ripples fanning out from the stern as the ship slowly disappeared into the horizon along with the sun.

8

He did leave us that summer on one of his usual trading trips, and we were left with the men sleeping above us and the shipmaster's sons in charge. This time, with their father away, the sons did not take the opportunity to call on the drunk widow. In fact, they hardly appeared in the square at all. They spent their time diving off cliffs or making bonfires in the valley or hiking up Mount Fern to spy on the men at the ruins. It was because they were keeping close watch, the baker told us. This did nothing to soothe his wife, who had taken to ringing her own bell in the square at nightfall mere minutes before the trumpet.

Now that Mother was at the pumice quarry, Giovanna and I were often alone. Is that why we ventured up through the forest to the valley below Mount Fern?

It was my sister who had the idea of crawling through the shipmaster's vineyards. Mother was sick of us bothering her at the quarry. She said it disturbed the other workers to see us in mourning clothes, wailing on the cliffs. She knew the manager of the vineyards in the valley – a widower whose wife had died of gout – and approved when Giovanna told her that we were helping him prepare for the harvest.

It was a lie, of course. At most, another game. We left early in the mornings, like Mother, wearing calico smocks over our dresses and straw hats too big for our heads. We crossed the square with a lantern while it was still dark, and climbed up the hill, through the forest, which was cool and wet at that hour. The air smelling of plants and fire ashes and flowers – woody and smoky and sweet.

We would arrive at the vineyards as the sun was rising. When the heat was too strong, we napped on the grass underneath the large oak tree right outside the shipmaster's house. Giovanna would openly stare at his windows, but I could not bring myself to look for fear of seeing the shipmaster's wife.

It was there, in the vineyards, that I began to learn things from someone other than my sister or mother. The widowed manager was the first person to talk directly to

me about the men. He explained that they were prisoners – murderers, liars, thieves, and much worse. He
said they had been rounded up from the mainland and
brought to our island without the shipmaster's consent.
I remember being shocked that anything could happen
on our island without his permission.

Giovanna, too, began to whisper things in my ear –
things I knew nothing about.

She told me that Mother had not been born on our
island, but on one of the smaller ones in the archipelago
with not a single tree on it, only rocks, and that the
people on that island lived solely on fish. Our mother
was young, she said, not much older than us, when our
father spotted her on the shore mending fishing nets
and knew immediately that he wanted her to be his
wife. Mother was happy, Giovanna said, because she
hated that island. When the day came, she got on his
boat with her meagre possessions – the shell necklace,
a red-and-white-striped dress, her favourite rock – all
wrapped in a scarf. Her family died that winter in the
famine, and she never went back.

My sister told me all of this with a smile. She started
asking me questions. Had I noticed, for instance, that
the widows on our island were shrinking? It was true
that the widows in our village and the older ones at the

port were not much taller than us. She said that Mother, too, was getting smaller and smaller, that one day she would be as small as a baby and that she, Giovanna, would have to take care of her, just as she had taken care of me. Perhaps she would dress Mother in my old baby clothes and tie the too-small bonnet around her head. *But why is she shrinking?* I remember asking. It had something to do with not having a husband, Giovanna was sure of it.

On those warm June afternoons, when the horizon looked blurry from the heat, Giovanna would fill my head with so many images that I would not be able to sleep.

She told me that the shipmaster had left that summer not on a trading trip, but to meet with *the swan people.* They were people, she explained, who had human bodies but long, thin necks with white feathers, beady eyes and black-and-orange beaks. She said that the shipmaster's cane with the goose head had been a gift from the swan people, who worshipped geese, even though they ate them.

How could I possibly nap after that?

Giovanna lay on the sheet underneath the oak tree and shut her eyes. Her breath became heavy. Her nose made a whistle that told me she was sleeping.

I was the only one awake, so I was the only one to see it. That afternoon, I saw a naked man running in the valley with nothing but a sack on his head. He zigzagged his way down the slope while the shipmaster's sons followed from above. In the middle of the valley they tackled him. The sons pulled him up by the arms and removed the sack to slap his face. The sun caught his honey-coloured hair, making it glint. I recognised him from the port. And the sons were laughing. They were patting him on the back as they marched him up the path.

It was hot. I was unsure of what I had seen. I went over to the well and dipped my handkerchief in the barrel of water – just like Mother had shown me – before tying it around my neck. The cool water dripped down the inside of my dress. I liked the feeling.

I never told Giovanna what had happened. I was alone with it. And when the trumpet sounded later that evening, while we were sitting at the table with Mother, I wondered about the naked man and what had happened to him, and then I looked at our mother and imagined her in baby clothes and my bonnet.

9

The rumour made its way down from the valley to our village. During the shipmaster's absence, a whole vineyard on Mount Fern had withered. With the harvest only a few months away, the waste made the shipmaster furious. When he found out – so went the whispers – he hit his eldest son on the head with a shovel. The baker was quick to dismiss this version of events. He spoke instead of a tussle between the son and one of the prisoners – one of the *rats*, he said – at the ruins on Mount Fern. I knew then that he was talking about the naked man. He told us that *the rat* had been caught at the port early one morning trying to escape. At this, he was incredulous. *Nothing gets past the shipmaster*, he boasted.

At first, we did not dwell on that withered vineyard. We were distracted by the news that the shipmaster had returned from his travels with a kind of magic box. That was what we called it, Professor, a magic box. It was a mechanical contraption encased in leather with a crank sticking out at the side, and it was said to make images that moved.

In the square, a patchwork of white linen was tied between two trees. Everyone brought chairs to sit in front of it. The shipmaster even organised for his piano to be brought down from his house – an opulent undertaking. The men from our village carried it on their backs through the forest while others followed behind pulling at the ropes attached. They were singing and grunting as they made their way down. Keys jangled. Notes clashed. The priest from our village – who, it was no secret, harboured musical aspirations – was given the task of retuning it.

When night fell, we were sitting in the square waiting for the shipmaster to arrive. His youngest sons appeared first, in their blue, buttoned shirts, and then the others, including the eldest, who did indeed have an eyepatch over his right eye. No one said a word at this, but there were whispers when the shipmaster's wife appeared with her hair in a new style – no longer twisted into two snails at the nape of her neck, but piled on top of her head into what looked like a giant bow. Instinctively, we looked at the drunk widow, who, on account of her tallness, was seated at the very back. She was slumped in her chair, her legs not tucked neatly underneath, like Mother's, but wide apart. At last the shipmaster appeared, wearing a stiff white shirt, his purple silk scarf and long black trousers. He was carrying the box, which had been wrapped in a woollen blanket. He did not address us, but simply motioned to his manservant, who took the box and set it up on a stand behind us.

How can I explain how it felt? When those images first appeared, our excitement gave way to fear. Most of us had never seen a photograph before, let alone one that moved. On the linen strung up between our trees, we saw ghosts and leapt from our chairs. Figures in black and white appeared. When we moved to touch them, our hands went straight through. The shadowy fragments of their bodies reflected on our skin. They were in the air, more malleable than dust. And the shipmaster was laughing at us, really laughing, as he called us back to our chairs, as he helped up one of the widows who had fallen to the ground. Beside me, Mother's hands were shaking on her lap, even though it was warm that night. The backs of my legs were wet against the chair. The palms that lined our square were still. There was no wind, not even a gentle breeze.

The priest began to play the piano. New images appeared. A young girl playing with her doll, a man with a crown on his head, a volcano erupting violently. Lava spewed in front of us and we looked instinctively at the volcano on the island opposite – only to find that its amber specks were fizzling no more than usual. The shipmaster remained silent in his chair. His thoughts unreachable. If he had not been responsible for making those images appear, the square would have erupted into chaos. For that was what was happening before our eyes on the linen between our two trees: chaos. The priest was now playing a frantic tune as the ghostly figures ran from the lava. There were furious flames. The young girl with the doll was crying. Big drops fell down her face. She was scared and we were scared and then the image disappeared and everything went black. White words appeared, but we could not read them. The tune changed. The priest's playing became softer. The volcano was gone. We saw a man and a woman meet in a garden and embrace passionately. It stirred something in me.

Time stopped. Who knows how long had passed before the film finished and the patchwork of linen became a patchwork of linen once more? A dream-like sleepiness had engulfed the square. We saw in the dim lantern light the iron benches under the trees that we sat on, the baker's blue shop, our yellow church, the mermaid statue, the sundial, the balustrade where we looked out at the sea and the black-rock beach below. Our square. We had forgotten where we were. It all appeared different. All of our usual things were now mixed up with the black-and-white images. I felt a gush of wind. How long had it been blowing? The palms above us were now dancing. We left the square that night in a daze, not speaking to one another, forgetting, for a moment, even where we lived.

We took our chairs home, but the patchwork of linen remained. It stayed like that – strung up between our trees – during the tumultuous months that followed, became increasingly dirty, stained by the birds. One of the ropes loosened and it drooped. Sometimes it flapped in the wind. Still, no one dared to take it down. I think we were scared, too superstitious to interfere with any-thing related to those images that moved, which seemed both real and unreal to us.

10

The next evening in our village, the talk turned to the withered vineyard on our mountain; how the green leaves had suddenly turned brown. Nobody knew the cause. The manager from the valley had gone to see the vineyard in question. He had hiked up Mount Fern and walked among the ruined vines. He had seen for himself the dry, dead leaves and the tiny, shrivelled grapes. *Unsalvageable*, he had said. In the square, we formed a circle and all sorts of theories were put forward. We spoke of the sun, how it had been much too strong early in the summer. There was talk of the quality of the soil, which was usually more fertile on Mount Fern. There was talk of the wind, of weeds, of the humidity and fungus, of known predators (like eagles) and other possible pests, until one of the fishermen stood up from where he had been sitting quietly on the bench and said in a small, croaky voice that surely it must have had something to do with the prisoners. He cleared his throat. It had been a poor fishing season so far, he explained, with only a meagre amount of swordfish, and this, too, was thought to have something to do with the arrival of the prisoners – if only the bad luck they brought to our island. No one dispelled the suggestion.

We were superstitious people – as you well know – and I admit that I still find it hard to shake certain illogical beliefs. They persist, Professor, even though I left that island long ago and have spent most of my life within a culture that does not have the mind for them.

Sometimes, I look back at my childhood and see forewarnings of what was to come.

II

One morning soon after, Giovanna and I came across our priest alone in the valley anointing the vines with his aspergillum and aspersorium. He was flicking holy water and muttering in that language of his. The act itself wasn't odd, only that he had chosen to carry it out in secret. We were usually involved in such rituals. We had the feeling that what he was doing was private, so we watched him from behind a shrub. When the priest reached the end of the valley, he made his final motions and slunk into the forest.

We found the widowed manager in the shipmaster's storehouse, cleaning the insides of barrels with a mixture of salt and lime. We helped him wash the empty bottles, then stacked them in the sun to dry. He went walking through the valley, stopping to inspect a leaf or a cluster of pale-yellow grapes. Two months remained until the harvest. The vines looked exactly as they should, he told us, and yet we could tell that he was nervous. He kept calling us by the wrong names. Mid-morning, when Giovanna went twirling and accidentally smashed some of the stacked bottles, he yelled at us to go home.

We returned to the square. Out on the sea, I could see the fishermen coming in, their lanterns still lit and swinging. The water looked grey, almost white, and their boats seemed to glide across it like open scissors against a piece of silk.

Outside his shop, the baker was boasting to one of the widows. He was telling her that he had spoken privately with the shipmaster, who had admitted his concerns about keeping the prisoners on our island. *Who knows what they are capable of?* the baker said, and his eyes were bulging then, almost coming out of his head. The widow beside him was chewing her morning hunk of bread, yelling, *It used to be a calm place, such a calm place!*

In the alleyway behind the baker's shop we came across our neighbour, the drunk widow, large and brooding in only her bedclothes, attaching a pair of ram's horns to the top of her door. She was winding rope around the horns and when she noticed us behind her, she stuck out her tongue and shut herself inside.

As that moody day unfolded, storm clouds gathered in the sky – dark and rumbling – but not a drop of rain came. The humidity was high. Even our eyelids were sweating.

That night in bed I woke to what I thought was our neighbour strangling chickens – high-pitched, gurgling cries – when really it was Mother yelping in her sleep. I rubbed her back until the noise softened, then rolled onto my belly. My bladder was full and bursting. I climbed over Giovanna and took the lantern out into the alley, swinging it wildly to scare away the lizards while I squatted to pee. I looked up at the sky, which was full of grey clouds, then at the dark sea, where I saw a light flashing. It pulsed in rounds of threes. The moon came out from behind the clouds, and I saw the shape of a ship on the water. It looked black and white, like something that might have emerged from the shipmaster's magic box.

12

I have told you already that I had no sense of the world outside the archipelago. The world was our island. The world was our square. It was the alleyways above the fishing dock, Mother's fingers stroking our hair, the black rocks on the beach, the yellow church, the baker's blue shop. Now a picture of life beyond the archipelago was forming. It was a composite of those black-and-white images, prisoners from the mainland, the swan people with the feathered necks that the shipmaster secretly met. You must understand: I had never left our island. Had never even seen it from the outside on a boat. Mother had strictly forbidden us from stepping onto any sea vessel.

I had seen that ghostly ship, and then the fishermen returned one morning with the news that a steam yacht had anchored at the port. Apparently, it belonged to a foreign nobleman. A woman from the market walked all the way to our village to describe him to us. He was a short, stocky man, she said, with skin as white as our pumice cliffs and a little paunch at his middle. He wore handsome leather boots, but his shirt was frayed at the sleeves. He was travelling with a group of sailors, and had bought a whole basket of prickly pears for an unfathomable price.

Of course, we were curious about this man. We wanted to walk to the port so that we could see his steam yacht. But soon the shipmaster's manservant arrived in our square looking frazzled – his long hair windswept and his face all sweaty. He went inside the baker's shop where the two of them whispered. When they came out, the baker told us we ought to avoid the nobleman until the shipmaster understood his purpose for visiting our island. The fishermen took this to mean that the nobleman might bring more bad luck. They were immediately spooked. They yelled at the woman who had sold him the prickly pears and she went off in a huff.

Later that afternoon, word came that the nobleman had rowed ashore and was walking in the direction of our village, taking the path that went up and down the cliffs, which none of us ever used because it was too dangerous. The fishermen grew flustered. The priest ushered us inside the church. He suggested we pray, but once inside, the baker locked the doors, and then he stood there, bent over, peering through the slits in the wood.

It was quiet inside. The faint smell of cinders. The pews creaking each time one of us moved. The baker's wife begged her husband to tell us what was happening, and he told her to shush; he could see a man coming. A pale man, he said. One with a little paunch. We sat there, in the dark, listening to the baker whisper what the nobleman was doing, saying things like: *He is looking at the sea, he is touching the statue, he has a menacing face, he has gone into the alleyway, he has returned, he is looking through the windows of my shop, he is crossing the square.* And while he said all this, I had an image of a stout nobleman with a menacing face carrying out the actions relayed.

Soon, we heard muffled voices. It was the nobleman's sailors. They were circling our village, so the baker said, knocking on our doors and peering through windows. *What do they want?* the baker murmured. And then, after a while: *They've left.*

That evening, the nobleman returned to his yacht and stayed there. We heard that he was ill. The feeling

among the fishermen was that the nobleman was carrying a curse.

We did not see him again for two weeks, and during
that time more vines began to wither. The manager
from the valley had once again hiked up Mount Fern.
He told us that most of the vines on the mountain were
dying. There were only a few patches where the leaves
and grapes looked healthy. We asked him about har-
vesting those grapes early, but it would not do, he told
us, because the grapes were not yet sweet enough. Our
wine was a sweet wine, he said, tearfully, and time on
the vine until the middle of September was what made
the grapes so sugary.

It was August. The wildflowers that shot up during
the spring on the unshaded parts of the island were
now scorched and looking like bits of straw. When the
sun came up in the morning, it was already hot and
blinding. We rarely left our houses after lunch. Mother
would return early from the pumice cliffs and close
the shutters. The three of us would lie on the bed, not
emerging again until the light was waning. Then we
would walk up to the square, the sky a dusty purple,
and sit on the benches looking at the sea, hoping for a
cool evening breeze.

13

When the nobleman recovered from his illness and came ashore, people began to talk about his wealth. He had given the widows at the port gifts of expensive lace and was paying one of them a large sum to cook his meals. Whenever he went to the market, he never questioned the price. It was true that he went about in torn clothing and an old hat, but he did wear those handsome boots – there was much talk in our village about his boots – and he had that steam yacht and his noble title. *The Count* is how he introduced himself. There was talk that he might be richer than even the shipmaster himself.

The priest thought we ought to embrace him. But the baker revealed that the shipmaster suspected the nobleman of travelling under a fake name. He instructed us not to speak with him about private island matters, especially the vines. The fishermen stood firm in their belief that no one should look him in the eye. To do so, they said, would risk transferring the curse.

We heard that he was making images of our island – sketching our boats and caper bushes and cliffs. He even sketched the women walking by him at the port. Mother thought this indecent, yet I secretly wanted to be sketched. I thought about twirling past him at the market, like Giovanna and I did in front of the workers at the quarry. But when the drunk widow was seen talking with him, it was looked on disparagingly. We took to throwing rocks at her house.

All the while, the nobleman and his sailors were going to the port and the market and the farms asking questions, such as what we ate, whether we could read, what work we did, whether we had ever left the island.

Perhaps you know about this nobleman already, Professor. Perhaps you have read his books. He came to our island with his sketchbooks and his questions, and he went out walking in the peak heat of those August afternoons and soon his pale face had turned red as a cherry. There was talk that he wished to stay. He expressed his desire to live on our island to the widows at the port. Yet he left us in a manner of weeks, and I still don't know why.

14

At the end of every summer, our priest led a procession asking for a prosperous harvest. The shipmaster's sons would carry the saints from our church all the way down to the fishing dock, where they would glide on the water. All of us children dressed in white. It was a serious affair, followed by a feast that began in the afternoon and went on late into the evening.

That year, we prepared with the knowledge that the shipmaster was upset about the vines – those grapes that had shrivelled before they were sweet enough to pick, which the baker was now referring to as *some form of sabotage.*

In the morning, Mother took us down to the stream with the fishermen's wives to wash. Dresses were smoothed over, hair untangled, dirt scrubbed from feet and fingernails. We all put in effort. Still, we were surprised to see the baker's daughter standing outside the church with flowers in her hair, looking – Giovanna said – as though it was her wedding day.

Inside the church there was an overpowering smell of citrus, and I imagined the priest, the evening before, on his hands and knees scrubbing the floor with chloride of lime. I pictured his cassock all wet, feeling light and woozy each time he rang the bells, and the pleasure that must fill his chest when he heard the clanging. He was seated at the organ when we arrived, playing a solemn tune.

I don't remember much of the service, only that Giovanna and I bowed our heads when we were supposed to, as we always did. When the time came to lift the saints – who looked worse for wear from their yearly swims – the shipmaster's sons gathered at the altar. The eldest was still wearing his eyepatch and he winked at Giovanna with his visible eye. The shipmaster followed and then his wife, who was wearing a white lace veil that covered half her head.

Down at the fishing dock, the tide was crashing loudly, and the priest's cassock ballooned out. The widows held on to their kerchiefs. The saints took their dip.

Afterwards, the women returned to their houses to collect the food they had prepared. They went back and forth with baskets carrying large loaves of bread, bowls with boiled octopus, roasted peppers, salted capers, sautéed chicory, anchovies in brine. The shipmaster's cook and manservant had arrived in the square hours earlier, pushing a wheelbarrow between them with a large pig inside – shiny and hairless and skewered through the middle, ready to roast. Now we could smell it. The drunk widow, who had not been to the service, appeared in her evening gown, hovering around the table where the wine pitchers were placed.

The sun shone blindingly, hitting the sundial in our square and bouncing off the white walls of our houses. The air was warm and filled with smoke. The mood was jovial. Suddenly, we were hungry.

We sat down to eat, and the baker proposed a toast to the shipmaster's health. We raised our glasses and applauded him. The shipmaster seemed to be smiling, and we were happy because it was important that the feast was a success. He was urged to speak and so he did, rising from his chair at the head of the largest table, all of us falling silent. He took his time, looking at each of us and then at the sky, gathering his words. He addressed us as his *friends*, his *family*, and spoke of changes on the island and the difficult winter we would likely endure on account of his loss of several vineyards. *An odd occurrence*, he called it, *a sad waste*. He paused again and looked at our faces, as if he was searching for any admission of guilt, and we looked intently into his eyes because we wanted to make him believe that we were not the ones responsible.

He went on to say what he always said at our feasts. That our island was the greenest, that we had been gifted a bounty of resources, that our women were the most beautiful in the archipelago. And as he said this, I looked around at the women – including Mother – with their chins tilted towards him, as if each one believed his comment to be addressed to them and them only.

He did not mention the nobleman, or the prisoners, and we dared not bring them up either. We did not want to spoil the occasion. Were we wondering about them and what they were doing at the top of Mount Fern that very moment? No, not then.

It was late in the day, and we had been drinking for some time. All of us, even children, would drink wine at the feasts. Drinking was only looked down upon if it was done in the grotto. Wine was like water, equally precious. It was viewed as a gift from our island – something pure. Something that could make you strong and healthy. Mother was drinking it and I was sipping mine and it made us feel warm and mirthful.

The shipmaster's wife left with his manservant. When night fell, most of our village was dancing. The fishermen huddled together at a table, singing their rhyming songs with dirty lyrics, and no one covered our ears or went to scold them. I was walking around the tables, picking up any glass with a little wine left. It was sweet and I was sucking it down.

At the edge of the square, I could see the baker's daughter leaning up against a tree while the shipmaster's sons pushed on her breasts like they were buttons. She was squealing – in laughter or pain I could not tell – and so I walked away and came across the baker on the floor holding his armpits for safety while the fishermen knelt down to tickle him.

Mother was looking at the shipmaster, who seemed to be staring at her, too, and when he got up from the table and walked away, Mother followed him.

They went behind the church, and when they thought they had disappeared from the rest of us, they embraced. They embraced the same way I had seen in the film in our square. I moved closer. Saw arms moving, but I could not see their heads. The shipmaster's hands were gathering up Mother's black dress so that I saw her legs and the white of her undergarments.

I returned to the square to find Giovanna, unsure

if I could tell her what I had seen, whether that was allowed, whether that was a betrayal of Mother, only I couldn't find her in the crowd.

Everyone was gathered around the roast pig, tearing off strips with their hands and licking their fingers, their eyes all glassy, and the skin around their mouths shiny.

The baker hoisted the pig above his head and said he wanted to taunt the rats at the top of Mount Fern. Suddenly we were in the forest. I was in the middle of the crowd. Up front, the baker was leading the way and crying out, *I'm a mouse, I'm a mouse.* I was tugging at dresses and pulling the hair of any child in front of me that resembled Giovanna. *We are rat catchers!* the baker was yelling, and we were bumping into one another and the trees, too. Someone was biting. Every now and then, a little yelp. A nip on the arm or the waist or leg or even the buttock – it must have been a child – but not one could tell who it was. We were yelping and everyone was laughing, but when we got to the valley the mood shifted and we fell silent. We saw the shipmaster's house in front of us and the full moon above, clouds racing past. Mount Fern stood tall behind it. An impossibly large shape against the blue-black sky. Too daunting and difficult to climb. The baker sat on the ground with the pig on his lap. He began to cough. Everyone idled around. No one wanted to climb the mountain. But no one knew quite what to do with themselves either.

15

The fishermen found the rowboat the next morning near another island in the archipelago that was so small it did not have a name. A black slab of rock – that's all it was. One sole tree at the top with spindly branches, not nearly enough leaves for shade. There was no life on that rock. In the rowboat they found a lantern and a compass. No clothes. No one swimming nearby. No sign of the prisoner who had gone missing the evening before.

The fishermen towed the boat back. We watched from the dock, expecting to see the escapee, whoever he was, suddenly sit up, but he never did. The boat was truly empty. And the fishermen were crossing themselves. They were scratching their bellies and rubbing their red eyes and telling us that the prisoner must have drowned, only they couldn't find his body.

The sky was overcast, blindingly white, and we walked up to the square from the fishing dock, finding remnants of our feast from the evening before. Bits of pig meat, stained pots, stale bread, empty wine jugs. The fishermen stood at the balustrade surveying the green-grey sea and the clouds that hung low on the horizon, talking about the tide, the possibility of a storm, and the body of the prisoner that must have drifted. The women, including Mother, sat on the benches looking up at the baker, who was saying that the prisoner's death was a sure sign, that it was proof of his guilt; that he must have been the one responsible for the vines. He urged us to muster a vivacious appearance around the shipmaster, who would, he said, be rattled that such an escape had taken place under his nose.

The night before, when we had finally climbed into our beds, we woke only a few hours later to the church bells ringing and the sound of the trumpet. In the soft yellow light of morning, the shipmaster's eldest sons appeared in doorways, telling us to go up to the square while they searched our houses. *Search for what?* Mother had said, but, of course, we knew already that it must have something to do with the prisoners at the top of Mount Fern.

16

The long days of September, before the autumnal storms, used to be my favourite time on the island. The most festive period after spring. It was when the grapes were harvested and everyone should feel full and happy on account of having more money and the heat no longer making us crazy. Everyone on the island would help with the picking. The women from our village would strap baskets to their backs or balance them on their heads. I remember the thin cotton of their dresses, their kerchiefs tied over straw hats, their muscular arms all dark from the summer. I remember taking handfuls of the pale-yellow grapes to eat, walking through the valley and spitting out the seeds. I remember seeing the grapes laid out in the sun on bits of cloth and lengths of cane. Once they had dried and hardened, they were taken to the press, where they sat under a weight while the juice dripped down. The juice was transferred into large vats and left to ferment. In January, we poured the wine into barrels, but only on a day when the wind blew from the north.

That September, storm clouds gathered early. There was the threat of rain. Everyone was on edge. Everyone was nervous because of the ruined vines on Mount Fern and the prisoner who had gone missing.

Amid all this, the shipmaster's eldest son proposed to the baker's daughter. His family came to visit the baker at his home while we stood waiting in the square. When both fathers had formally accepted, the shipmaster hosted an impromptu party in his back garden, where music played from his gramophone and there was dancing, though no wine. Following the baker's instructions, we all tried to look relaxed and happy, even if we winced when we heard the sound of the evening trumpet.

The nobleman left our island without warning, and there were grumbles about this, especially at the port, because it was thought that we could no longer rely on the shipmaster for money.

When it came time to pick the grapes, the mood was sombre. It was thought to be a meagre harvest, though it would seem bountiful in the years to come.

I do not have to tell you, Professor, about the awful harvests that followed; how each spring the vines would shoot up – the leaves looking bushy and green and full of promise – only to turn brown, as if it were suddenly autumn. One row of vines would look afflicted, then it would quickly spread. The stems turned chalky white. Each year, we tried to revive them. You have written of our methods. You know that nothing worked. Within five years our island became unrecognisable, and then we all left.

17

Professor, I woke up this morning and thought to ask: have you ever heard the sound of a volcano exploding? Suck your breath in, then make a 'da' sound quickly, moving your tongue down from the roof of your mouth, expelling all of the air you have drawn into your belly. Do you feel that shuddering? Are your lungs reverberating? Do you feel the brief panic of no longer having any breath? That is what it feels like when you first hear it. But after that ungodly thud there is the most magnificent silence, smoke clouds expand in the sky, and it is beautiful.

PART TWO

ARCHDUKE

1

When I made that first journey, more than twenty years ago, to the island of S, I had never been so far south in the Mediterranean – on the cusp, as it were, of the Arab world. I had not tasted the food from that region, had not heard the dialect, was yet to learn about the people and their habits, the volcanic activity, the animals, the rocks, the vines. But I was, of course, already a writer. Just one year earlier, at the age of nineteen, I published my first book – a slim documentation of Venice written in French and dedicated to my mother. *From your loving son*, I inscribed her copy using my very best steel nib and with no splodges.

My childhood had been a sickly one – I was sent to Venice to recuperate from the lingering effects of past infections, and the sea air and the salty water and the sunshine did bring me back to health. I spent my days lolling on the lido, floating in the Adriatic Sea, stopping to chat with the fishermen, sketching the cedars and magnolias. At night, I wandered the maze-like alleyways of San Marco, getting lost as I searched for somewhere to take a meal. Against orders from home, I stayed on until the winter and watched the city transform. The dull grey sky that replaced the endless blue one seemed to highlight the mould covering buildings, invisible to me in August. At one point, the turquoise canals appeared brown. One tavern I frequented flooded twice and the other patrons remained seated all the while, deboning their fish while the murky water lapped at their boots. Still, nothing could dampen my love for Venice. The abundance of beauty I found there was overwhelming, and it was this feeling that led me to write.

Seeing that first book come to fruition was thrilling. Publishing came at a considerable expense. For although I ordered only a modest number of copies to be printed, I insisted on the very best paper. I wanted the most rigid yet smooth paper, so as not to invite creases. Gold leaf for the cover. I commissioned the best illustrators to transform my humble sketches. I agonised over the layout. I wanted the book to be practical, yes, but I also wished to make it an object of beauty. Secretly, I envisioned all kinds of men deriving knowledge from it, just as I had learnt so much from my treasured books. Indeed, I put my heart and soul into that first project, and seeing its transformation from thought to object brought on a sharp pang of unbridled joy. And yet, the joy was fleeting. The joy was gone once I discovered the flimsiness of the spine, the tattiness of the pages, the too-loose binding. Upon holding the book in my hands, I saw that the precious gold leaf, in a certain light, re-sembled nothing more than an inelegant orange. Yes, I noticed these things, and I thought to myself that the book looked like a cheap pamphlet. A guide for frivolous travellers – interested only in superficial experiences – instead of what it really was: a study on the natural wonder that is Venice. Disgusted, I put the book in my drawer.

With time, I came to see this view as childish. Yet it remained true: I no longer loved my book. When I looked at it, I was struck by a wave of unexpected am-bivalence. The emotion was so strong that I could only look at it with eyes squinted; could only take in certain fragments. I tried to recall the time that had prompted the writing of the book in the first place. The sense of importance I attached to the book I now rightfully attributed to my time in Venice. But when I shut my eyes, everything that came back to me – the thick fog on the canals in the winter mornings, the faces of certain vendors at the Rialto market, gondolas gliding past at midnight with their lanterns flickering – all of it came from my rendering in the book as opposed to the original experience. Even now, when I remember that trip, I question whether I am only remembering the book version.

And yet, the experience did not deter me from writing another one. Twenty books, in fact. A sense of duty has something to do with it. Should a man not stray further than Venice? Having travelled far and wide, I long for the sensation brought on by an unknown expedition. My addiction in life, as Sisi always said, is travel itself. I sleep better on my steam yacht than I do on land – that is well known.

Two years later I was on my way to the island of S. But what drew me there? A hankering for warmer weather. An interest in the mythical history. Curiosity about the climate and the native botany on an archipelago so close to Africa. The desire to get as far away from home as possible. In Venice, away from family and other prying eyes, I found myself smiling madly as I walked down streets, feeling as though I had been released from some hidden burden. I heard myself speaking in a voice that sounded so unlike my own. I was very aware of myself and yet I felt anonymous. The experience appealed to me. I wished to repeat it. I had finished my studies in geography, philosophy and botany, and I proposed a trip to the archipelago in order to write a study – one, I argued, that might be useful to a man wishing to expand his land ownership further south.

The book I published about the island of S was taut and practical. I included only the information necessary to my purpose. As with the rest of my books that would follow, I included very little about myself. I omitted certain experiences. I held myself from view.

It is true that I have altered myself as I have sailed around the world; altered myself according to the place I have found myself in, to the people I have met. Indeed, I have both consciously and unconsciously changed the way I walk, speak, smile, laugh, what I laugh at, what I smile at, what information I relay about my life, what I think about that very information. Indeed, I have metamorphosed as I have moved across this world.

I was given twelve names at birth, and those twelve names have variations of their own. So in Austria, my first name is Ludwig. In Italy: Luigi. In France: Louis.

And so on. When I visited the island of S, and indeed when I travelled in other parts of the world, they knew me not by any of those names, but by my alias: the Count of Neuendorf, or simply the Count. I held up this farce, I admit, because travelling in such places often made me uneasy about my status. It seemed to me that I had to do away with my identity.

It caused me great grief when I found out, much later, that some of the subjects of my books did not like what I wrote about them. For I always approached the subject with such care. If I wrote about them, I can say now it was because I wanted to be them or felt that I was them already. And yet, precisely because my book was about them, it felt wrong to include my own feelings, my own subjective experience. Back then, I had a particular aversion towards those books which pretend to be about a particular subject, but are, in fact, only about the self that wrote them. I detested those books. I often felt the desire to wash myself after reading such a book. Now I see that it is impossible to write with such neutrality – that this kind of authorial neutrality does not exist even in scientific endeavours. The subjects of our investigations reveal our biases, and we expose ourselves through writing, whether we intend to or not.

I was a different man, a much younger man, when I first visited the island of S. That I encountered fear and suspicion, and that I myself left the island feeling fearful – I still regret. There are things that occurred on that trip that I have never relayed to anyone.

All of this, it goes without saying, is not intended for publication. These are my memories. Please, be patient with me. I am on my steam yacht. The ocean is calm. I am sailing south, far away from the archipelago, but if I close my eyes, I still might be able to draw her.

2

What I remember is that we arrived stealthily, by moonlight, and yet when we docked there were already people waiting for us at the port. A stout man carrying a lantern emerged from a carriage and approached one of my men on shore. He introduced himself as *manservant to the shipmaster* and enquired after my reason for visiting the island. He extended the shipmaster's invitation for a meal and a bed for the night at his home. When my man rowed back to us to relay the message I gave my answer promptly. *Kind sir, there is no need for that. I am well equipped on my steam yacht and profess to enjoy sleeping in my cabin.* I thought this would satisfy him. Only later would I learn how wrong I had been to refuse. There is no point in dwelling. Truthfully, I was annoyed by the request, given before I had even the chance to step ashore.

On the pier was a small ball of a woman with a basket of prickly pears at her feet. When I signalled that I wished to try one she flapped her arms excitedly. She cut out the flesh from its spiky exterior and handed it to me on the knife. It tasted sweet, like a melon, with little seeds of dark burgundy. Without my men, I understood very little of her dialect and so I mimed with my hands and lips how much I was enjoying it. She offered me another. I bought the whole basket – not yet knowing, of course, that they grew wildly all over the island. I often found the pink flesh of the fruit rotting or smeared across the rocky paths.

That first morning, I went walking on the small beach by the port. The sun was rising. The water reflected the orange and red hues of the sky. The trees above me on the mountain were rustling. The island smelt of jasmine, wood smoke, brine and dung. Then came the wind – famous in the archipelago. It whipped my cheeks and made a delightful whooshing noise, sounding, I thought, like an army of small children attempting to whistle.

On my way back to the port, I saw farmers leading donkeys down the hill, their pack saddles laden with vegetables, hessian sacks and green glass bottles. A market was now bustling, and my men bought supplies:

bread, tomatoes, capers, olive oil, salted fish, wine. We took the rowboat back to the yacht and tasted the island's bounty. When I finally returned to my cabin I went to bed in that hazy state one gets in when one has spent one's normal sleeping hours awake. My head felt heavy. I did not think much of it. Too much excitement, perhaps. I closed the curtains and wrapped my linens around me. As usual, the sea rocked me to sleep.

3

I slept peacefully, content in my cabin, after those first hours on the island. The only sign of ill-health was a dull ache in my legs – sore muscles, I thought, from my long walk in the morning. When I opened the curtains, I was surprised to find the late-afternoon light. I filled a sack with supplies: my sketchbook, pencils, ink, some prickly pears, my paring knife and the surveys I had prepared with questions for the inhabitants. I gave it to one of my men to carry and we rowed to the port. On foot, we set out in the opposite direction of the light-house, keeping close to the water. When the shoreline became inaccessible, we hiked up steep hills on paths less worn. How they got their donkeys and carriages up there I could not imagine.

As usual, my men were trailing behind me. It is not

that I consciously walk so fast, but rather that I find it so tedious to stroll. Little steps, head down, hands behind the back – it all reminds me of laps around palace gardens, of small talk in parlours about scandalous marriages, the cost of recent renovations, whether there might be afternoon rain. Oh, how I loathe to stroll! How I hate to be kept at the bumbling pace of an ambler. I have short legs – it is true – but they have always taken quick strides. Indeed, for every long stride a man takes, I take two little ones swiftly. Or, at least, I did back then.

It was late July when we arrived in the archipelago and the sun, in the late afternoons, felt oppressive. Sweat was gathering at my neck, in my armpits, around my groin. The sea below seemed to taunt us.

As I walked that day, I felt an urgent desire to document the flora and fauna I was seeing before me – some cultivated, but most of it wild. Dwarf palms, fig and carob trees, rosemary and caper bushes, olive trees and, of course, the cactus bearing prickly pears and the Malvasia vines – little vineyards I encountered on every slope. I had my sketchbook and pencil. I could have made some rough drawings. I could have examined the vines more closely. But I wanted to enjoy the walk. I wanted to absorb the island. I had that feeling I always have when travelling: I wanted to revel in the present moment and yet I was anxious about capturing my response to it in case it slipped away. No, I cannot say with any certainty that I stopped to inspect the vines on that first day.

Something curious occurred. I came upon a small village that was completely empty. My men were trailing far behind me. I walked across an empty square. All the doors on all the little white houses were closed. Yet when I walked through the alleyways, I found signs of life – woven baskets with washing, a broom, a half-cleaned cooking pot, a child's bonnet. I heard no voices, could smell nothing cooking, though surely it was time for lunch. Even the church doors were firmly closed. I stood at the balustrade and something stirred behind me. I turned to find a large linen sheet strung up between two trees. It made an ominous flapping sound – the only discernible noise until I heard my men jostling one another. When they got to the square, I instructed them to knock on all the doors. No one answered. Somewhere, above us on the mountain, I thought I heard bells, then nothing.

We found stairs that led to a beach below with black rocks. The sound of them being dragged by the tide was pleasingly methodical, like the chanting of monks. At the shore, we removed all of our clothing and stumbled over the rocks. The water was silky and warm. My men swam out while I lay floating on my back looking up at the sky with my ears submerged – the sound of my breath magnified. Something caught my eye on the cliff. A man was standing at the balustrade at the edge of the square above, watching us. I dipped my body under the water, raising my hand to greet him, and thought I saw the man nod in response. It must have been the shipmaster. I did not allocate much importance to it at the time.

Later that night, in bed, my skin felt itchy against my bed linen. The throbbing inside my head returned. My body was sticky. I opened the windows of my cabin, hoping for a sea breeze, but the humidity of the day had not broken and the sky was thick with clouds. No stars. I thought to myself: rain would be nice. Now and then, as I had trouble dozing off, I thought I heard the sound of thunder. Only the rain did not come.

4

I woke up the next morning feeling sweaty, believing it to be the result of too much sun the day before when, in fact, it was a fever brought on by flu. For there I was – there but not really there, as it goes in dreams – lying in my cabin while the sun streamed in, but also, simultaneously, back in Prague in that cold classroom on the top floor of the Kinsky Palace with my old philosophy tutor, Doctor Strobe. It was snowing outside, and Strobe was looking intensely into my eyes. It was a game he liked to play when our discussions hit an impenetrable lull, often after a disagreement. Who would look away first? It was meant to test my character, or perhaps display the strength of his own. He had a stony demeanour and often lamented my tendency of becoming – in his words – *overly dramatic* during our lessons. The man did not blink. Did he ever weep? It was as if he slept with those grey eyes open. I thought he was dear to me. A father figure of sorts. But once I let my guard down, those eyes came out. I felt that he gleaned things about my life under the guise of philosophical interlocution.

I was young and I admired him. For he had published a great many books. They lined the shelves behind him in the classroom; indeed, his books looked down on us while he taught, enriching everything he said by making his words verifiable, imbuing them with unequivocal proof. For there they were – his words – sitting proudly above us. Should he want to prove something, he had but to reach up and take down one of his books, open it to the correct page and place it on my lap. Which he did, often.

Early in the course of our lessons I asked if I might borrow one. It is true that having come to study with him, I found myself completely out of my depth. I could barely spell. It was a great source of shame to me. Although I could converse in a number of languages, I had trouble writing in them. I could feel the shape of the word in my mouth, knew how to carry it, but the letters themselves appeared fuzzy. No, I did not know how to spell. I might as well confess that it was during my period of study with Doctor Strobe – and his incessant penchant for teaching via humiliation – that I developed my now much-regretted habit of illegible penmanship. I know there has been talk about my writing. Before I studied with Strobe, I had the most perfect cursive writing. I took pleasure in lining up the words. But Strobe's habit – of taking my essays and reading them aloud in a painfully slow manner, stopping each time he found a mistake, annihilated any joy I took in writing. He would read my work in a voice reserved solely for this purpose, using a little inflection at the end of each sentence, casting doubt on each of my statements, turning them into questions. He would stop, haltingly, whenever he found a spelling mistake. Then, with the exaggerated acting skills of a carnival clown, he would attempt to read the word the way I had spelt it, even though he knew, from the context of the sentence, which word I had attempted to call forth.

I began to dread our lessons, finding myself unable to sleep the night before, having nightmares in which that high voice of his appeared. I am not lying when I say the man almost drove me to a nervous breakdown. Now that I am older, I feel almost sentimental about my memories of Strobe. With age, he has become harmless. But at the time it made me prickly with nerves. I can still see him now, striding back and forth across the room reading aloud, while I, squirming in the armchair, look longingly out of the window of the fifth floor, desiring to jump. Not to kill myself, you understand, but to escape his bizarre theatre of cruelty.

The point of all this – to return to my secret – is that I began to write badly. Indeed, I no longer wrote; I scrawled. Pages and pages of indecipherable writing. I saw it as a sacrifice I had to make for self-preservation. For Strobe could no longer read my essays at all, and although he could chide me at length for my terrible penmanship, the onus was now somehow on him. He would read aloud and haltingly stop, no longer in a theatrical way, but of his own accord. Indeed, he could no longer read, and it rattled him.

In my cabin, during my feverish episode, my dream had shades of this – Strobe reading aloud, chastising me, making me feel as small as possible – but what I recall most vividly is the stare. For I was sitting in the armchair opposite him, our gazes locked, and I knew, I just knew (as one knows in dreams), that I needed to relieve myself but could not. I knew I was dreaming, and yet I still felt that my dignity was at stake; that my very pride depended on staying in the chair and holding his gaze, not blinking, not turning away first. My bladder was full. Strobe's eyes were fixed on mine. The little white hairs inside his nose were dancing. He was a very loud breather. A voice inside my head spoke to me: *You can no longer hold it in, why not let go?* It happened instantly. My whole body unclenched, it was warm inside my trousers and then I felt tingly, full of relief. The warmness quickly turned cold. The acidic smell of my piss cut through the mustiness of the room. Strobe looked down. For a second, I saw his face soften; saw something that looked like confusion, perhaps pity, then it became taut and unflinching once more. *Go clean yourself up*, he said. And this was the very worst part of the dream. For I had to get up and navigate the wetness between my legs; walk with them parted awkwardly, like a cowboy, across the room as he watched.

And, of course, as I dreamt this I really did relieve myself, only I did not know it immediately. When I woke up, everything was drenched – myself, my bed linens, the mattress – in sweat as well as urine. Some of my men went ashore in search of a physician and returned with a group of elderly women dressed in black. Widows. They were small women with faces worn by the sun and long black scarves tied around their heads. They stripped the bedding and removed my clothes, washed me with water infused with lemon, whispering to one another all the while about my body in their dialect, of which I caught certain words. Specifically, they mentioned my hairless chest – *Like a young boy*, one of them said. There was something else about my manhood, I am sure of it, though I was too delirious to protest or enquire after their meaning. Truthfully, it was comforting. Not so much the comments about my body, which are always jarring, but to be undressed and scrubbed clean. To have my hair washed and combed. To have my chest rubbed. To be brought large bowls of hot water with floating eucalyptus leaves and have a towel draped over my head while those gravelly voices whispered soothingly in my ear, telling me to *Breathe, breathe*. To have clean bed linen and to lie down, feeling light and oddly lifeless, while the ocean rocked beneath me. To go in and out of sleep and wake, always, to find one of the widows' faces above mine, smiling. Once, I opened my eyes to find one of them signalling for my mouth to open and before I knew what was happening, she had slipped a mulberry inside. She even called me *a beautiful boy* and I can honestly say that I enjoyed it; felt happy to receive it. For it had been so long since I had been called that. Deep down, I knew I was not a beautiful boy; that I had never been thought of as beautiful. Indeed, *beautiful* was not a word often used in my family.

Then came the chills. I lay in bed, shaking, and was thrown back to scenes of my youth. The large palaces with their endless, extravagant, lonely rooms. The clopping sound of the maids' shoes as they walked up and down the halls. The soft hands of my nanny, Concetta. The garden in Florence with its winding paths of white gravel, the tall cypress trees and Mother's medicinal cave with the large clam bath where she retreated whenever she felt ill. Being whisked away to Switzerland, age ten. The snow. The fountains that froze over in winter. Gooseflesh. Steam emerging from my mouth with each breath.

The problem with Switzerland is that it is cold. The problem with Austria is that it is cold. It is the kind of coldness that makes even your bones quiver, and it does not exist in the Mediterranean. Winter comes, of course. There is the strong wind in the archipelago, very brisk from November onwards. But the bone-quivering coldness, I am certain, does not exist. And yet there I was: lying in bed in my cabin, shivering, though they assured me that the air outside was warm. How I longed for it. I felt I was losing time. From my little window, I saw the moon rise and fall and yet I did not know how many days had passed. One of the widows spoon-fed me some fish broth and I felt only hotness in my mouth. I longed for my senses to return. Longed to breathe easily. I wanted to be outside and exploring the island. I wanted to be hiking up the volcanoes of the other islands, the thrill of death at my fingertips – a thrill that is only truly thrilling when one is perfectly healthy. I was left alone for long stretches while my men went ashore each day, as I instructed them to, in order to interview the inhabitants – the very work I wished to be doing. I felt alone on my yacht, isolated, my dreams and memories all on a loop. After a while, even the widows stopped visiting.

I say all of this because it no doubt contributed to the fever-induced decision I made during my illness. I had been weakened, it is true, in the mind as much as the body and it made me nostalgic for home and for Mother. I was lying on damp sheets in my cabin, hearing the ocean and other night sounds, sometimes jovial ones coming from the port, longing for her. But Mother, of course, would never come, and so I did the next best thing and wrote to Sisi. I practically leapt out of bed when I had the idea. I thought of Sisi's smile and her adventurous side. *Please come*, I wrote to her, careful not to mention my sickness or to beg. *Leave that sour-faced husband of yours behind and join me*, I joked. I described the islands and their various qualities. I embellished, of course, but only a little. I did what I had to do to make her jealous. I wrote of waking to dolphins outside my cabin window greeting me with early-morning salutations. I wrote of sweet plums and soft peaches and the exoticness of the prickly pears. I wrote of the changes in light reflected on the rippled surface of the sea, its inviting temperature. I mentioned the youthful sailors that passed through the islands. For I knew that these were the things that would draw Sisi so far south and not, in fact, love and worry for her beloved cousin.

I entrusted the letter to one of my men and went back to bed feeling satisfied. For the first time in two weeks, I had accomplished something. I experienced an almost unbroken sleep. A few days later, I began to feel like my old self again and in my excitement of grabbing that old self with both hands, I forgot all about the letter.

5

I got in my rowboat and shooed away my men, eager to be out on my own. I felt little pinches in my arms – a sign of weakness – and yet I rowed harder, not wanting to embarrass myself in front of my men, who were watching me from the yacht. It was the first time I had left the cabin in two weeks. I rowed frantically until I had rounded the curve of the coastline and my men had disappeared from view. Only then did I stop to catch my breath and cough up mucus from my chest. My throat was dry. I was already sweaty. I reached into the sea and ladled out water to splash on my face and neck. My little rowboat was rocking. I steadied it and admired the view of the island from this new angle. Her two green peaks – those two dormant volcanoes – covered in vegetation that sloped at different angles.

They looked like two large cakes with scalloped icing of forest green. I took deep breaths, envisioning the good air filling up my lungs, as I had learnt to do as a child on my health cures.

I rowed further until I came upon the same black-rock beach we had swum at when we first arrived. The shore was empty, but a little boat was near one of the caves, and in it were a whole family fishing together. A rush of confidence overtook me. I called out to them using the dialect my men had taught me, but they made no response. The father was smoking a pipe. Of the three young boys, one of them was holding what appeared to be a grouper. The mother was sitting with a baby on her lap drinking from her breast. I surveyed them gingerly. Had I been born on this island, I thought, I might have sat in a boat like that, happy, holding a grouper in my hands. I might have fed from Mother's breast instead of Concetta's. They had not seen me and so I cleared my throat and called out once more. The husband looked up at me and then at his wife. Immediately he began crossing himself, as though I had caught him mid-prayer. I waited for him to finish, then called out once more, complimenting his fine fishing skills. He took the grouper, still flapping, from the young boy and threw it in my direction. The fish landed in my boat. I heard the wife curse. The young boy looked confused. Wanting to rectify the misunderstanding, I went to throw the fish back, but the slipperiness and the flapping loosened my grip and it fell into the sea. We all looked down. The husband began muttering in prayer once more. Feeling embarrassed, I picked up my oars and rowed away.

I wanted to go as far as my tired arms would allow. I followed the coastline until I saw mountainous jagged rocks emerging from the sea. I rowed closer to touch them and felt little electric vibrations all over my body. I thought of the Greeks sailing through these islands; of sirens and pirates; of Charybdis – the whirlpools once thought to be a sea monster off the coast of Messina. We had passed them on our way to the archipelago and heard the womanly wailing from which the myth arose. I was caught in this loop of thoughts when there was a sudden splash and a boy broke through the surface of the water next to my boat. I looked at him and then up at the group of boys above, waiting to jump. The oldest looked not that much younger than myself. They were laughing. I wished, not for the first time that day, that I had brought my men with me. It is hard to be confident when one is alone and up against a group. Still, I could observe them. I could draw their bodies, if only in my mind. They were scrawny, yet muscular. They did not have the same brawniness – that thickness around the middle – of the young men I knew back home. No, these boys had nimble limbs. They twirled in the air. Their backs arched spectacularly. Their necks were elongated, like swans. Their beauty was identical. Perhaps they were brothers. They were trying to get my attention. I realised their intentions too late. A little wave capsized my boat. I felt the rude shock of seawater up my nose. When I came up for air, the younger boys were doubled over and some of them were even pointing as they laughed. I choked a little and tried to smile. I turned my boat over and straddled it.

Rowing back, I felt a sudden sense of urgency. My leisure hours had been filled. I had whetted my appetite for observation. I had seen the island from another angle. I could feel the wheels of my consciousness working. All my life I have felt – with pleasure! – the familiar tug of my work. It is like this: I have my fill of images and thoughts and then something tells me it is time to start. I wished to take advantage of the feeling. Back on my yacht, I closed the curtains of my cabin, letting in only a little light. I could scarcely believe it was the same room I had been in, days earlier, on my hands and knees in the middle of the night wondering if death was upon me. The room had been aired out and tidied. Indeed, it was a different room now. An urgent room. A room in which to get things done. I sat at my desk, happy to immerse myself in the images. Happy to put my mind to something. It had all been gathering momentum. I described the rock formations – their twisted shape, how they looked like long candles with dripping wax. I described the red rock of the cliffs and the wild cacti with its prickly pears. I wrote of the boys jumping, and made a note to enquire about the bathing rituals of the inhabitants.

I looked through my cabin window. The port was very quiet. The sun was just about to leave the sky. There was a stillness outside that matched the stillness of my mind and I lay down on the bed savouring the feeling. It was the first time I remember being conscious of hearing it. Somewhere in the distance, the long, sombre tones of a trumpet rang out. I thought it a lovely, if melancholic, sound. Only later that night did my men inform me of its purpose.

6

Was I curious about the prisoners? Only as much as I
was about the other inhabitants of the island, some of
which, my men had told me, were cold and difficult to
speak with. Yet I thought that the people at the port were
becoming warmer, more familiar with my presence.
Faces at the market broke into glorious smiles whenever
I bought something from them and offered a new snip-
pet of dialect I had learnt the day before. I found myself
performing all kinds of generous acts. If I am honest,
it was my wish to be liked wherever I travelled. A bad
interaction with a local could turn my mood for days. I
suspected that my status at the port had been improved
by my good relations with the widows who had nursed
me back to health. There was an easy intimacy between
myself and those older women that came from them

seeing me so vulnerable. They were not formal with me at all. Indeed, one of them used to wink at me when I greeted her at the market.

I remained anxious to make up for the time I had spent ill in my cabin. I set out on those August mornings at first light. By midday, I would be melting in the heat. I told my men to stick to the lower parts of the island so that at least we could bathe in the sea. Still, heatstroke was a recurring affliction. I spent three nights with wet rags covering my face. From then on, whenever I stopped to sketch a shrub, or a boat, or an empty cistern, I did so with one knee on the ground and the other propping up my sketchbook while one of my men held out the parasol to shield me from the blinding rays.

In the evenings, there was really only one place where we could take a meal. Like other establishments at the port that catered to service, it was a private home. A small house belonging to one of the widows, Emilia, who set up benches and chairs outside her front door anytime a ship anchored and the alleyways were suddenly dotted with uniformed sailors. Emilia was elderly – just how old she would not tell – and she was incredibly short (her head reached my stomach), yet she raced back and forth from the kitchen as she carried small bowls of salted capers or a warm salad made with aubergine; wild greens cooked in garlic; rabbit with fennel and beans. She took a particular liking to one of my men, Antonio, and would clap her hands with joy whenever she saw him coming, often referring to him as *the healthy boy*. A reference to his appetite, and yet I could not help thinking it was also a joke against me.

I would sit on Emilia's empty benches in the late afternoon and watch the day draw to a close. Young women with baskets balanced on their heads passed by me as they made their way home from the port. Their beauty needed no emphasis and yet they adorned themselves with jewellery made from shells; intricate ornaments featuring cypraea that the women in my family would no doubt find gauche. I thought their necklaces and earrings to be inventive and authentic – an indication of their connection to the sea. Indeed, I wished to know more about these young women, but local etiquette would not allow it. They were unmarried, to begin with, and they lived in the secluded fishing village my men and I had found empty on that first day.

One woman was the exception to this rule. I came across her one afternoon at Emilia's, and was struck by her unusual dress. Imagine a peasant dressed in an opera costume of dirty white lace. She looked as though she had been plucked off the stage at La Scala. She was a solitary figure, going about her business at the port without a chaperone, without greeting anyone. My men told me that she was a widow who had rejected the rituals of mourning, and that her husband had died years ago in what some locals thought were mysterious circumstances. This woman had gloriously wide shoulders. She towered over the other inhabitants. She walked right up to the bench and sat opposite me. She had long eyelashes that fanned her drooping eyes, which were dark brown, almost black. I introduced myself and asked if I might interview her. In a voice that came from somewhere deep in her diaphragm, she informed me that *he* would most certainly not be happy about it. I was confused, as I had thought her a widow, and explained that I could call upon her husband first and ask permission. She smiled. I had begun to explain my study of the island when she reached across the table and touched me, tenderly, on the nose. *I find you very interesting*, is what I thought she said before getting to her feet, not without wobbling, and retreating up the steep hill at the edge of the market. I had an impulse to follow her and so I did.

I walked at a distance, keeping that ridiculous dress in my line of vision, up the hill that led to the valley – a path from the port I had not yet taken. I saw the vineyards, planted all over the slopes, but there was also an abundance of ferns; poplar, oak and strawberry trees; jasmine and bougainvillea. I had no time to stop. The woman had disappeared into the forest and I walked quickly to keep up with her, weaving through the trees, until she reached the fishing village, which looked so different to the ghostly one I had encountered. Now, it was brimming with life. Children dressed in white dresses or shorts with no shoes or shirt were banging on cooking pots with little sticks. They were yelling at the woman, and then they, too, began to follow her through the alleyways. I was at the back of the line. Women were standing at their front doors, gesturing to one another as I walked past, averting their eyes, and the children were taunting the woman, poking at her dress with their little sticks and calling her names while she rushed inside a small house. One of the little girls even threw a rock.

Walking back through the village, I crossed the square, where a group of fishermen stood gathered at the balustrade looking out at the sea. Not one of them returned my greeting. Only the priest, standing at the open doors of the church, bowed his head in return. Night was coming on. I walked quickly through the forest, absent-mindedly taking the wrong path. I got lost. I retraced my steps. I heard the trumpet and then other muffled sounds. I looked up and saw, way ahead of me, what looked like a large grey animal. It was a group of men in grey tunics. And two boys, no older than fifteen, were following them, rifles strung over their backs. I recognised them from the group of brothers I had seen jumping from the cliff. As they disappeared among the trees, I heard a voice behind me whisper: *It's the prisoners.* I turned to find a lanky farmer – one I recognised from the market. He was holding his hat in his hands and he gestured to the group, said something about a prisoner – only I could not catch the meaning of the word. *I don't understand,* I said, and the farmer repeated the same word emphatically. I shook my head: *I'm sorry, I don't know what you're saying.* He spoke again; the language he used was coarse. It was a word I recognised. He could tell I understood. He was waiting for my answer. I could not make out the expression on his face. I gestured to the canopy of trees above us and the last shards of light disappearing from the sky. *I do not have my lantern,* I said, and with that, I turned and walked back to the port.

7

When I was thirteen, I was whisked away to an alpine spa town to undergo hydropathic treatments. I had been ill years earlier with tuberculosis, yet there were other unspoken reasons. I was too small, my joints were weak, I made a wheezing sound while breathing, my knees were peacocked, my voice was nasal, my posture was lacking, I had a tendency to follow the maids around the palace and once I took Bertha's skirts and slept with them in my bed, I wept often, I was always asking the wrong questions, I failed to explain myself, I did not respect the silence of the afternoons, I loved Mother a little too much.

One of our carriages was packed in the middle of the night and they bundled me into it. Me and my trunk. One of the nannies – decidedly not Bertha – came with me. She held my hand and told me to try to get some sleep as the carriage traversed the rickety paths. We were heading north-east, further and further into the cold, and soon I could feel the sting of wind on my face – the kind of coldness that comes just before snow. I had on my fur coat. A beaver hat. Woollen socks, two pairs. I looked out of the window but all I could see were dim flashes of green – the trees lit up briefly by lanterns. The nanny's voice was comforting and her gloved hand was enclosed in mine. The sound of her breath became louder and louder until it turned into faint snoring. Who was she? Her name escapes me now. It was one of the younger ones.

We travelled down roads that eventually became smooth, the wheels of the carriage falling into a pleasing rhythm, and only then did I sleep. When I woke, we were passing through villages. The land was flat, and the palette had changed to brown and beige. I saw a windmill. A little bridge. Wooden barns. Some mountains in the far distance. We stopped at a farm and I was given a glass of fresh milk, some bread to dunk. I had to relieve myself and was taken into the living quarters where I saw, huddled together in one tiny room, a family of fourteen warming their hands over a fire.

On we travelled until it became green and hilly once

more – the horses grew fatigued on those narrow, windy roads.

At the gates of that yellow hotel which housed the guests, the manager of the spa was waiting to greet us. My room was on the top floor. It had red walls, a large fireplace, a brass bed with thick woollen blankets. On the table in the corner, there was a single glass and several large jugs – all labelled differently – containing water from the various springs. One was high in calcium, another brought on a laxative effect. My window looked out at the hills and the other hotels and at night I could hear, faintly, the streams of the springs and the fountains splattering, the screech of carriage wheels. My dreams were all water. I stayed there for two months.

And I enjoyed it, did I not? I liked the feeling of soaking in the thermal springs even though they let off a terrible smell. I liked the warmness that penetrated my bones. The shock of the icy water poured on my neck. The wire brush they dragged across my skin so as to stimulate my insides. The wooden clogs I wore in the tiled basement on my way to sessions. And the hotel robe – identical to those of other guests, though mine had been embroidered with my initials. I was well known in those squishy corridors. The youngest resident there. The other men – all of whom I remember thinking looked close to death – were most likely the age I am now. Where was their life? I remember thinking at the time. What had happened to it? What had made them leave it to bathe, like babies, in the hot and then lukewarm and then cold water of the alpine region? It was hard to keep my curious eyes averted from their naked bodies. One man of noble standing was bald and on his shiny head I always found a safe place to focus. I spoke to no one.

Until, of course, one morning a boy of about my age appeared. He walked into the dining room looking like a scared rabbit. He had a habit of rubbing his thumb and index finger together – an anxious twitch. I do not know why his blond hair and his nervous demeanour set off something so strong in me. It was a pull that I tried to resist. He was not a beautiful boy. In fact, there was something decidedly ugly about him. And I think that his lack of beauty, in retrospect, elevated myself (also lacking in beauty, though less than he) so that a safe and inviting dynamic grew between us. He was no talker. They sat him at my table, just the two of us, and he said not a word. I got the feeling he was intimidated by me. Weeks passed before I asked him to come walking with me in the grounds of the hotel, and when I did – heart racing in anticipation of his reply – all he did was put down his knife and fork and nod. The sound of our boots crunching in the snow was deafening. Such was the silence between us.

I knew, from hotel gossip, the relevant facts about his family and status. I wanted details. I wanted him to trust me. I thought he had much to divulge. *Tell me about your mother*, I would say on our walks. And he: *Oh, there isn't much to tell*. It was infuriating. I would talk about my own family so that I could end with: *And your father, is he the same?* only for him to reply: *More or less*. Or: *I guess I really don't know*. His ambiguous responses drove me mad. It is no exaggeration to say I became obsessed with the boy. The less he talked, the more I imagined his history, the deeper I envisioned his emotional terrain. I was drawn to his shyness, which I interpreted as tenderness. His blankness, which I mistook for mystery. I see now that he was a canvas on which I could paint all of my desires.

Early on, I enquired after his bathing schedule and would time my walks in those wet corridors so that I might bump into him 'unexpectedly'. I did this even though I sat with him three times a day in the dining room, neither of us talking, delicately cutting up a potato, a string quartet playing in the corner.

Later, he began to visit my room – which was far better than his – in the evenings. The two of us often sat by the fire, hardly speaking. Sometimes I would stretch out on the bed and read a book, one hand propping up my head. Only I could not read. My eyes would scan the words, I would turn the pages, but I would take in no meaning, so that I kept having to turn back and reread what had come before. Even if I had my back to him, his presence would reverberate in the room, making it impossible for me to concentrate. After a while I began to stare at him – openly stare without even attempting to hide it – as he fiddled with the fire iron or sat in the desk chair with his impassive face turned towards the window, and I would ask him: *Albert, what are you thinking about?* And he would keep his eyes on the trees outside and say something like: *The veal the cook makes back home.* Or: *The cherry strudel we had for dessert.* Or else, he would turn to me, only a hint of emotion on his face, and ask: *Do you think there are wild boar in those hills?* His gentleness catalysed my ferocious need for action. So that one night, as we lay on the bed – me with my book and him staring at the ceiling, rubbing his thumb and finger together – I pulled one of the woollen blankets up so that it covered us. Something about the darkness made it possible. I could not see his face, but I could hear his breathing. And I felt it keenly – the pull between us. I leaned in and so did he. The intensity of that kiss is something I have not since experienced.

8

I have read over these pages. It is not coming out how I intended at all. Writing is like sleeping; you loosen the grip on your consciousness and suddenly old friends and foes appear in the dark. A vaguely familiar face emerges from obscurity and announces its unexpected importance in your life. A memory you may have wished to forget rounds a corner and waves its hand. Subjects to which one has given little thought in daylight hours come up recurrently. I have known writing to be magnetic, pulling me in directions I have not willingly wanted to go. I have spent the last twenty years planning the precise route of my travels, and it is difficult to surrender to such an unknowable course.

I must admit that it is also strangely alluring – this relinquishing of my life to the page. I have long kept logbooks while travelling in which I note my reflections. They paint an incomplete and puzzling picture. A sentence here, a small sketch there, quotations, titles of works I intended to seek out once on land and inside the pleasingly lit anonymous halls of some foreign library, not to mention the sheer amount of incomprehensible marginalia. This document – I hardly know what to call it – feels entirely different.

It used to be, in recent years, that when I sat down to work I would find myself up again: walking absent-mindedly around my cabin, washing my face at the basin, staring out of the window at the ripples in the water, selecting an opera to put on the gramophone in the hope that it might put me in a mood conducive to writing, opening the doors of my glass cabinets so that I might touch the precious objects there. Whenever my hand drifts over the treasures I have collected – masks, porcelain figures, pressed flowers, pinned butterflies, miniature paintings – I find that it lingers, always, on the section that houses the geological specimens. In par-ticular, I am drawn to the bit of pumice I procured from a beach on the island of S all those years ago. I like the feeling of its porous surface on my fingertips – the small groove that fits my thumb just right. I have often felt the need to keep the rock on my desk while I write. Lately, the ritual has not been necessary. All the research my work usually revolves around – maps, encyclopaedias, public records, interviews, sketches – seems dispensable. I am alone with my memories and that is all. I am in my cabin at night smoking my pipe and listening to Rossini or I am waking in the morning and marvelling at the way the sun obscures the line between sky and ocean at that hour, and then, mere moments later, I am wandering around other rooms of my life.

Part of the allure in writing this, I have to suspect, is that it cures the loneliness. These pages have brought me back to a time of my life when I used to surround myself with people. My men – from Corfu, Verona, Mallorca, Messina – have long returned to their homes to live a more anchored life while I have kept on going. I have travelled for some time now with only a skeleton crew and Antonio is the only one who remains from the original group. Those once-rumbustious days on board are far behind me: the parties, the singing, the dancing, the long nights of discussion, the arguments, the physical altercations between my men – usually stemming from accusations of malingering – and the long resulting silences, especially when we were far from land, for that does indeed do something to one's state of mind. The annoying habits of each of them, the changes in mood from too much drink, their astonishing lack of hygiene, the tricks they used to play on one another and, increasingly towards the end, me, whom they called *oversensitive* which never ceased to hurt my feelings. I miss it all. I long for it even though none of it would appeal to me now. Even though I grew sick of it quite suddenly. It was like this: something inside of me snapped and I no longer wanted to be around my men, or indeed anyone. I could not handle even the most basic human interaction. I began to fantasise about being on my own. I thought: *If I have to see his face when I wake up in the morning one more time.* I thought: *What I would give for uninterrupted silence and a little space.* I thought: *I cannot stand this meaningless chatter.* I thought: *I am no longer happy around my men and I can no longer hide it.* One by one, upon my instructions, they left. I did not regret my decision. I felt more at ease than I had in a long time. I was able to work again and felt calmed by it. These days, when I am lonely, when I find myself desperate for distraction from my own thoughts, when I lament the long hours that stretch out in the evening, I try to remember how many years I spent craving them.

The problem is this: I am drawn to people. I want to know everything about them. I want to sit with them, converse with them, laugh with them, learn about them, confide in them, have them confide in me. Then, quite suddenly, I want to be rid of them. I have no doubt that my travelling life has facilitated this pattern. I have docked my yacht and fallen for the face of a stranger. I have invited outsiders to my cabin. I have even taken them with me when we have set off. I have had more than my share of impassioned goodbyes at various ports – have stood on my yacht and waved as I watched some beloved become smaller and smaller until they were no more than a dot on the shore, imperceptible from all the other dots.

People are a source of great pleasure in life. They bring spontaneity into what would otherwise feel like a scripted affair. They shock you out of yourself. They change you. But they also cause great pain. It is un-complicated to love a mountain. All that is required is that you turn your attention to it. Nature asks so little for what it provides. I sought out beauty from a young age because I realised that the world was full of it – that there was an endless supply in the natural world just waiting to be discovered if one was curious and willing. I was surprised to learn that there are many people who are neither curious nor willing at all. Whenever I encountered these people, it felt as if I had told them they had an extra limb and they had replied that they had little interest in using it. I may have denied myself certain things in life – I may have turned away from people – but I cannot say that I ever closed myself off to beauty.

When I was a child, an intense fear of death gripped me. It came from early illnesses, assassination attempts on my family, the constant threat of war. That mankind was violent and unpredictable, that someone might want to take your life and was utterly capable of it – these thoughts formed my very being. I do not know how to live without them. If I sought out anomalous company in my travels, it was because I thought those people to be unaware, or in the very least unfazed, by notions of danger. They seemed to be able to live without falling into spirals of dark thoughts. I was scared of my own mind. I tried to surround myself with people who lived as though life were a series of beatific surprises. I liked having their energy around me. I hoped it would be contagious.

When I first visited the archipelago, I was practically a child. I had not yet grown into my face. I thought I had experienced loss and pain, but it was pale in comparison to what would later come. I was not weighed down. I felt very much alive. I was ecstatically happy and somehow oblivious to it. I had my yacht and permission to use it for my research purposes. I was going to travel the world. I was going to contribute something new to my family's legacy. I was going to have a different life – out here on the ocean – to the one that had been laid out for me. And so I did. But I cannot say that I was able to rid myself of various phantoms.

9

Most afternoons on the island of S I went by the postal office to check for news from home. I did so with ambivalence – I desired information yet was dreading any message that might command my return. There were several long correspondences – with old friends and various librarians – in which I was involved. Whenever I received a letter I would intend to wait until I was alone in my cabin so that I could savour the reading experience but found I could not manage such patience. Sometimes I read my letters standing at the dock or sitting in my rowboat while simultaneously composing the reply in my head – stirred by the images and thoughts and questions – only to then stuff the letter in my pocket and wait several days before actually responding, which by then often felt like an unwanted task.

At the end of August, I received a reply from Sisi to the invitation I had sent asking her to join me. It was curt and mysterious. Non-committal. Just two words on a golden sheet sealed with her wax stamp: *I might.* Very Sisi.

I thought of past adventures together – sneaking away from some formal gathering to traverse palace grounds, swimming in a pond in our undergarments, both of us inebriated and chasing the swans. I thought of Sisi's curiosity about the world, her knowledge of things I had not yet discovered, even though I was the one who had completed lengthy periods of study. I admired her unwavering confidence. In an argument, she would not budge, whereas I was always doubting myself.

I folded the letter neatly and began to row back to my yacht, feeling the sun on my face, looking out at the other islands, imagining my cousin sitting opposite me in some ridiculous travelling hat bought specially for the occasion. I saw myself directing her attention to the little thuds heard in the archipelago, explaining that they came from the volcanic islands in the distance, that there was no need to worry. I began planning an itinerary of activities, assigning the relevant ticks and crosses, for there were some that would not suit Sisi.

She was not an early riser, to start, and was known

to be squeamish when it came to food. Where, I wondered, would we take our meals? Sisi would certainly not appreciate the warmth and authenticity of a place like Emilia's, would not even try the rabbit. Indeed, when Sisi ate at all it was food that had been prepared precisely to her liking. Then I remembered the entourage she would no doubt require in order to travel. She would bring her handmaids, of course, and her tutors, who would no doubt question me about my research – work that I wished to keep private. I even imagined some of them writing letters home in which they gossiped about me – everything from my clothes to my relations with my men, to my manner of speaking with the locals. I could almost hear the accusations. *Ludwig is embarrassing himself in front of the peasants. Ludwig is squandering money. Ludwig is going about in torn clothes and a common hat. You should see Ludwig! How fat he has become.* No, none of it would do. How had I forgotten how much I detested the company Sisi kept? They were small-minded, ignorant, truly ugly people who talked of things they knew nothing about. I felt repulsed by the very idea of their presence.

I was thinking all of this, and by the time I got to my yacht I was sweating and angry about the letters I imagined Sisi's entourage sending. I did not want those people in the archipelago. I did not want them to taint the place. I knew that I would not be able to work while they were around, that I would feel self-conscious and scrutinised by their mere presence. And what about Sisi herself? She was not someone who could fall into the rhythm of things. She was not someone who could temper her tone. I often loved that about her. She had an inability to control her facial expressions around people she quite obviously disliked – a fact I had always found refreshing. She could be cruel. She, too, could be gossipy. I only liked it when it was us against the others.

On my yacht, I ignored several questions from my men and went straight to my cabin. I had created an unwanted dilemma for myself. I felt the beginnings of a headache approaching. I paced around the room, wondering how I could untangle myself from the trap I had set. I grew sad. I rationalised. I loved my cousin. I missed her. I imagined her arrival and, because of the dramatic way I was feeling, it took place at night, her boat coming to meet mine under the moon, her long hair blowing in the wind, our embrace. Only the image did not calm me, it brought to mind another problem: that hair! It almost touched her ankles. Washing it was an all-day affair. I had seen her, once, sitting in her chair surrounded by women with brushes, practising her French while the rest of them giggled. No, I could not have Sisi here. It would ruin everything. I sat at my desk and quickly wrote my reply. *My dearest, beloved cousin. I am heartbroken to tell you that there is no time for such a joyful occasion as a visit. My research is almost complete and soon we will be moving on. It pains me to send such a message when I was so utterly desperate to see you. Write me at our new address. I will ask Antonio to send it to you when we dock.*

I returned to the port immediately to post the letter, wishing to take advantage of my worked-up state, knowing that if I left the matter overnight, I might not be so brave as to post it the following morning. I left the letter with the clerk and went to sit on the rocks.

The sun was setting – a sight so extremely beautiful that it made me feel ill in the stomach. I had become accustomed to the splendour of that particular hour on the archipelago, and I wondered if the pain in my belly was an indication of my guilt at depriving Sisi of such beauty. A wave of uncomfortable reflections followed. Was I meant to be alone? Did other people find human interaction so fraught? Was I incapable of selfless love? Sunsets – with their theatrical intensity, their utterly unambiguous way of marking time as one travelled towards death – often prompted such sensitive thoughts.

10

I was feeling sorry for myself – a frame of mind I ab-
horred in others. I was sitting on the rocks having just
posted my letter and watched the sun dissolve into the
sea. Children were singing at the port. Their parents
were calling to them. Over the years spent on land, the
brief periods in which I lived in foreign cities, this was
the particular hour I liked to take my evening walk –
just before night fell and everyone was returning home.
I would look up at apartment windows with curtains
not yet drawn and find rooms glowing with light.
Walking down empty streets, all the bustle of the day
having come to an end, I would revel in the sensation
of being surrounded by people but truly alone. If I felt
sad, I was also filled with a kind of quiet calmness. It
blanketed my mind after a day of drowning in my own

thoughts. Domestic sounds would escape through open doors. Snippets of conversations, someone practising the piano, dogs barking, dinner bells ringing, children screaming – I took it all in. Streetlights around me would blink to life as the lamplighter, another solitary figure, went about his work. Once in a while, I would look up to find the face of an elderly person standing at their window, returning my gaze. I would tip my hat and quickly move on. If I am honest, such a sight often ruined the experience.

On the island of S, the lighthouse was flickering. The sky was electric blue. Tiny white crabs were scurrying sideways, disappearing into holes. The tide was unusually low. I heard jovial sounds – laughing, yelling, singing – coming from all over the island. An accordion, somewhere in the distance, was playing an upbeat tune. It contrasted pleasingly with my melancholy mood, by which I mean it deepened it, allowing me to wallow. The low tide revealed a path along the rocks and I walked along it, stumbling in the near dark, lured by the sound. Somewhere on the way I sliced my palm on a sea urchin and stopped to rinse the blood. I rounded a corner and there it was: a secluded beach with boat wreckage, black sand shimmering from the moon and the glow of the lighthouse above. Long, moss-covered ramps led up to a grotto. Shadows were dancing across the walls. I could smell urine and wine. The accordion was coming from inside. I walked up the ramp. At the mouth of the grotto, I stood with my hat in my hand. There were peasants dancing and sailors scattered on the floor. The accordion player was at the back, his elbow jutting in and out as he pushed and pulled the bellows. Beside him, a short, muscular man was frantically beating a tambourine. I felt a tug on my trousers and looked down to find an elderly sailor beckoning me to the ground. I sat beside him and he raised his bottle. He told me it was the island's liquor – sweet and syrupy and very strong. I drank it in one gulp and was immediately given another. Soon my ears were warm.

The night stretched out. I searched sweaty faces, finding none I recognised, until the peasant I had met at Emilia's appeared in her opera dress. Her presence did not go unnoticed. The whole grotto clapped and cheered at the sight of her. She weaved her way through the crowd, twirling her torn dress with the lace tendrils, curling her fingers in the air as she danced to the back, where she stopped, hallowed by her large shadow on the rock wall. A hush fell. For a while, everyone was silent. She began to sing with deep vibrato and no accompaniment except the sound of the waves outside. Her voice swelled. Her song – thick in dialect – was sombre and moving. I only understood a few words and yet I felt I understood it all the same. We held our silence until the last note rang out. Then she collapsed on the ground. I saw someone hand her a bottle. New sounds emerged. It was a game of sorts. Everyone gathered in a circle and was encouraged to sing. A sailor beside me sang a dirty tune usually reserved for the company of other sea timers. A farmer, who I now recognised from the market, sang a folk song about his allegiance to the land – his voice breaking, then becoming more confident, so that by the end he was practically yelling. There was a look of triumph on his face when he finished and treated himself to a large gulp, and I was gulping wine, too. I was drinking whatever was poured into my little sticky glass. I was calling out to the others in the circle, pointing to peasants and demanding that they sing, hearing my own voice become louder. Then, softly, surprisingly, a sailor lying on the ground outside the circle began to sing a lullaby. I was entranced by his song, which was about a mother caring for her child. We fell silent, just as we had when the peasant in her opera dress sang, not making a noise or moving until he finished his song. The grotto erupted with applause.

Bottles were smashed in excitement. The sailor was hoisted onto shoulders and paraded on the long ramps that led down to the beach. I followed, feeling wobbly. When everyone returned to the grotto, I jumped down onto the sand and walked to the shore to piss.

I saw him standing near the wreckage of old fishing boats – the sailor, the one who had been singing. He looked at me and I looked at him and I recognised the invitation. Recognised it from the docks in Venice and the shipyard in Barcelona. Neither of us uttered a word as we began walking, weaving between the boat wreckage, him leading the way, turning back to make sure that I was still following him. The lighthouse, far above us, was rotating while we walked, so that we were shrouded in darkness and then, briefly, exposed to light.

11

Everywhere I have travelled – if only for a brief moment – I have thought the same thing: I could stay. I could stay here and make another life. The thought is my opium. I have been chasing the feeling for forty years. You see a world in which there is nothing of yourself and you walk towards it with arms open. Only it will not have you, not truly. It will never accept you as one of its own. You will forever be an outsider who has chosen a new place to reside. Even on those other islands where I made a home, created new roads, commissioned statues, planted seeds, surrounded myself with the company of locals, I sometimes found myself walking along the shore – perfectly happy – to then suddenly wonder: *What am I doing here?* Such momentary lapses have the effect of vertigo. I try to steady myself and my thinking, but the feeling is too strong. I lose my sense of self. Shortly after, a depressive slump follows and I take to the sea. To be in constant movement is the only thing that cures this particular affliction.

I know that on the island of S, I had begun to entertain thoughts of staying. Of buying a house and filling it with my treasures, not abandoning my yacht but instead travelling only in the winter, heading further south for warmer climates, and returning, always, to the archipelago. It would be my base, a home of sorts. I would send for my books. Perhaps I would teach the women and children to read. I envisioned myself helping the little ones, walking around my garden, informing them of the proper names of each species of plant. I found such thoughts – of myself as a different person; a kinder person – invigorating. I imagined forming a strict routine: bathing in the sea in the early mornings and sitting down to work soon after, learning how to fish and becoming self-sufficient, even going out in the middle of the night and returning in the mist of the morning like the other fishermen. Perhaps they would warm to me. I imagined sitting on the rocks, smoking a pipe. Sending letters home at Christmas. *Greetings* – I would write – *from the most exquisite corner of the earth.*

My work on the island was ending. There were others to visit. It made sense to move on. In other words, it was safe to want to stay because I knew we would soon be leaving.

Of course, I did not realise this at the time.

I woke up on the beach below the grotto, lying among the boat wreckage, little waves lapping at my feet. My boots were gone. I was naked from the waist down. There was no sign of the sailor who had held me the evening before. Something that felt like a frosty burn was enveloping my head. My body was speckled with black sand. The sky was white. It was warm. The sea was choppy. I waded into it and swam out as far as I could. I looked back at the red rock of the grotto and the greenery of the mountains looming above.

Searching around the wreckage, I retrieved my trousers, but not my boots. I walked back barefoot along the rocks, smiling. The tide now reaching my shins.

When I arrived at the port, I was told by one of the market vendors that my men had been searching for me since dawn. Although it was early, he was already packing up his cart.

I rowed back to the yacht, where Antonio was waiting for me with the news that a prisoner had gone missing the evening before. They had found an empty rowboat, he said, anchored near an islet.

12

I spent the day and night in my cabin, lying in bed, my head caught in a cycle of thoughts and images: the sailor on the beach with the black sand, Sisi's possible arrival, the prisoner who had escaped – whether he had abandoned his rowboat. I was restless. My limbs felt heavy. I wished to walk. I wanted to feel the elements – the sun and the wind especially. I rowed ashore in the afternoon and found myself taking the more arduous track that wrapped around the cliffs. I did not bring my sketchbook. I had no supplies. I walked quickly – quicker than even my usual pace – until I was sweating and my chest was aching and I had to sit on a rock to catch my breath. I looked out at the sea. Felt the warm breeze. Heard the trees shaking above me – little broomsticks sweeping the inside of my mind.

Then I heard something else: church bells ringing as they do only in celebration. They were coming from the little fishing village. I followed the sound. By the time I reached the square, the bells had ceased and only the priest stood outside his church. He beckoned me over, telling me that a proposal of marriage had just taken place. The shipmaster himself had accompanied his eldest son to seek approval from the girl's father, the baker in this village. Now everyone was on their way to his property to celebrate. He lowered his voice and told me that he hoped the occasion would bring harmony to the island after what he termed *recent difficulties*. I thought he was talking about the prisoner and was poised to ask whether they had found him, before the priest asked if I would like to come in and eat with him.

Inside, the church was a humble place of prayer. The walls were white with blue trimming. Several painted wooden statues of saints perched above us, chipped here and there with the effect that some appeared to have only one eye or half a lip. The altar – with its lit candles and holy crosses made from cypraea – looked primitive compared to the grandeur I had seen in Venice. I was taking it all in when the priest invited me to sit in his living quarters while he prepared.

The room was small. A straw-stuffed sack sufficed for

a bed. There was a little table with two chairs, a dresser with a washbasin, and a modest collection of cooking utensils on a shelf adjacent to the fireplace. Some books stacked up against the wall. That was all. He insisted I sit down, and as I did he lit the fire, on which rested a pot of something already cooked and congealed at the top.

The priest removed his cassock, and I was able to properly observe him. He was a slim man with hair all over his chest and arms and none whatsoever on his head. At the basin, he washed his face and armpits vigorously. He took two glasses from his shelf and filled them with wine. He stirred the pot, explaining that it contained the remnants of his dinner the evening before, apologising that the meal would be a simple one. I assured him I had no banquet expectations and that I had been enjoying similar meals at Emilia's place by the port. He settled into the chair opposite me and raised his glass. We drank together and once again I tasted the sweetness of the Malvasia and felt a warm rush in the chest. The priest asked me what sorts of foods I had eaten while growing up. I was surprised by the question and thought for a minute before saying, tactfully, that while I had eaten all sorts, I preferred the food from his region; the simplicity of a dish with three ingredients and the array of fruits that one could enjoy. I was trying to reassure him that I did not look down on his island.

I studied his response, taking in his features – the big eyes and the petite lips, watching them break into a smile when he replied that he was not from the archipelago, but had in fact been born in the north. His mother and father died when he was young, he explained, and he was passed among his extended family until he finally joined the church. At the age of ten he had come to the south, but he still remembered everything from his early years in the north: the food, his family, the music. He seemed to be on the verge of telling me something. I wished for him to continue, so I said nothing. The fire had doubled in size and I could feel my cheeks growing rosy. We were all alone in his living quarters where there were no windows, and for this reason a confessional tone had quickly been established between us. *It is different here*, he said carefully. *I cannot easily display my other devotions.* I asked him, gently, what else he was devoted to, and he looked intently at the fire before meeting my eye and saying, with great sincerity: *I love meat and I love music.* I took a sip of wine quickly in order to suppress the smile that was spreading across my face. In all earnestness, he explained that no one on the island ate any meat, apart

from rabbit and, perhaps three times a year, a celebra-
tory pig. As for his love of music, he said, he could only
indulge it on suitable occasions. He knew that here, on
the island, he would never reach his full potential. I was
taken aback by his passion and by the confidence with
which he spoke of it. I asked him if he might consider
playing something for me. There was a small organ in
the church, he said, and then, not without a hint of
jealousy: *The shipmaster has many instruments at his house.*
I rose from my chair. *The organ, then,* I said, leading the
way back to the church.

I sat on one of the pews and he took his place. I closed
my eyes, heard the stool creak, some light coughing,
a long exhale. I recognised the hymn as he fumbled
through the first notes and then paused. He began again
from the start, only to stop once more. I heard his long,
exasperated sigh, some angry mumbling to himself. *I'm
sorry,* he whispered, and then, in a voice that cracked:
I'm so nervous. I opened my eyes. *Imagine you are on your
own,* I offered, and I got up and walked to the back of
the room to position myself in the shadows. When he
began to play, I noticed a change in the way his fingers
hit the keys. He was no prodigy. Indeed, his technique
was a little clumsy, yet he played with his personality. I
could feel it in his performance and I gravitated towards

it. When he finished, I applauded him loudly and made sure to tell him, several times, how wonderful it had been to listen to him, how unique his playing was, how I longed to listen to more. None of it was a lie, and that made it all the easier to say.

We returned to his living quarters and resumed drinking together with the familiarity of lifelong friends – his impromptu performance having deepened the rapport between us. In that cosy room, he ladled out bowls of soup, tore off hunks of bread from a half-eaten loaf and picked up two spoons, wiping them on a dirty rag before handing me one. We ate quickly and in comfortable silence. He refilled my glass and asked me questions. Where was I born? What did my family do? Did I have a sweetheart at home? When would I marry? I gave only vague answers. I tried to steer the conversation back towards him. He seemed frustrated with my replies. The tone changed. He pushed his bowl aside and began to speak to me of delicate matters concerning the social intricacies of the island. He seemed a little drunk, and I suppose by this stage I was, too.

He turned out to have – like most priests – an insatiable appetite for gossip. Indeed, he began to unburden himself of the many secrets he was required to keep on behalf of the inhabitants. I did not judge him for taking the opportunity to confide in me – an outsider – such sensitive information. I have often thought of the difficulty and restraint involved in holding on to so many personal woes – it is the very reason I do not take confession. I listened to it all with interest. It was scandalous, though not completely surprising, to learn that the shipmaster had fathered many children on the island outside of his marriage. The priest assured me that it was well known but not openly acknowledged, and that the children in question were unaware. He spoke of the shipmaster's generosity and his position as benefactor to many on the island. He owned most of the land. As such, he was held in unthinkably high esteem; both adored and feared. His liaisons with various wives of the inhabitants – mostly the fishermen and the farmers – had ruffled feathers and aroused suspicions for many years. This past summer, the shipmaster had angered some of the villagers, as they believed him to be responsible for allowing prisoners from the mainland to stay on the island since the spring. Two vineyards had died in quick succession since their arrival. Sabotage was suspected. The island was split in their thinking of who the culprit might be: the imprisoned men or one of the inhabitants themselves. Now that one of the prisoners had managed to escape, it was felt that the shipmaster was losing his standing on the island.

I wanted to ask him about the vines. But the priest gulped back his wine and said that he did not believe the rumours about me; that he could see that I was an honest and kind person. I shifted in my chair. *What rumours?* He went on to inform me of the shipmaster's belief that I was a spy. The thought was so absurd I began to laugh. The priest told me that my scholarly curiosity had been regarded with suspicion. I tried to rationalise with him. *What use,* I asked, *would information about the farming and fishing habits serve?* He said it had puzzled him, too, and reiterated his belief that I was not someone who set out to deceive them, but he added that my *recent activities* had given him pause. *Which activities?* I asked. Well, he said, I had visited the grotto. There were reports that I had been seen on the beach naked and not alone.

The room felt much too warm. I shook my head. The priest looked sheepishly at the table and apologised, saying he was not one to believe rumours. I assured him that I was not bothered by the talk – that I knew not to take it seriously. He apologised once more. He began to speak of the coming harvest and the possibility of storms. I could not follow the conversation. I told him it was dark, that I ought to be leaving, and he walked me through the empty church. It had changed immeasurably in atmosphere since his performance, given only an hour or so earlier. At the doors, he extended both hands and shook mine heartily.

13

We had arrived in the archipelago by moonlight and we left the same way. It was a coward's exit that I did not wish to take. But the revelations from the priest, the feeling of being watched, unnerved me to the point that I did not wish to formally farewell the island either. On my walk back that night, I could not shake the feeling that someone was behind me. I kept turning my head. The friendly faces that greeted me at the port no longer seemed innocuous. What had they seen, I wondered, and what had they said about me? When I reached my rowboat, I was in the depths of a melancholy mood. The island had changed. It looked different. Not the dancing trees, nor the dramatic outline of her two dormant peaks, could squash the bitterness I felt as I rowed back to my yacht. Sadness made me feel weak

– not a useful emotion at all – so I worked myself up with anger instead. I kept returning to the intrusion of privacy. I relayed the thought over and over. When I reached the yacht, my mood was foul. I ordered my men off the floor. I admonished them for drinking, even though I myself was quite drunk. I told them that we were leaving that very evening. I saw their confused faces and the glances exchanged with one another as they worked. I locked myself in my cabin and fell on the bed.

Machinery churned somewhere below me. I looked out of my window at the other islands as we pulled away – black lumps against the night sky and little spurts of amber lava. Finally, I looked back at the island of S. She looked so regal, a rare beauty. It would be years until I returned to her, and by then, she would be an entirely different place – one I could not reconcile with the memory in my head.

14

My sources tell me that the spread of phylloxera began with a humble botany enthusiast not unlike myself. A curious French peasant was sent rooted vines from his friend in California and happily planted them in his backyard. They arrived in a box lined with moss that had crossed several oceans on a steam ship. Had the ship relied on the wind to make the journey, the aphid surely wouldn't have survived. It jumped – the aphid – from vine to vine, starting from the Frenchman's backyard and spreading out across the continent, finally reaching the archipelago.

Imagine a tiny yellow insect. She lives in the roots of the vines. Indeed, her whole life will be subterranean, if that is what she wishes. All the nutrients she relies on to survive she gets from sticking her needle-like mouth into the roots and sucking. She reproduces asexually, laying thousands of eggs in her lifetime. And the vine, with nothing left for itself, begins to die. It changes colour. The leaves become dry. The whole plant withers. The aphid goes to sleep in the winter but awakens each spring.

15

When I returned to the island of S, all those years later,
there were no more prisoners. Another island in the
archipelago now served that purpose. The prisoners
there slept on vermin-infested straw inside the walls of
an old citadel. By then, phylloxera had wiped out all the
vineyards on the island of S, and most of the inhabitants
had left for the New World: America, Argentina, Australia. I was told that the shipmaster's family had been
the first to go, followed by the priest. I did not recognise
any faces at the port, and if they recognised me, well,
they did not show it. There were no sailors there. No
ships coming in and out. The whole island looked di-
lapidated after years of neglect. Children lingered in the
alleyways like stray dogs looking for something to eat.
Large patches of land where the vineyards were once

planted had been burnt – the soil destroyed by sulphur. I walked up the sloped hills, through the forest, down to the empty fishing village and the black-rock beach, returning to the port on the path alongside the cliffs, trying to revive the feeling I had upon my first visit, only it would not come. Again, I left the archipelago in a depressive slump. I took to the sea, where there was other beauty to be discovered. And I found it.

PART THREE

GIOVANNA

1

What if I told you voices come to me? What if I told you I am a vessel for the voices?

Late at night, this man – a professor – calls me. All I have to do is listen. Hold the telephone close to my ear. It is midday where he is. It is close to midnight here.

The first time he calls, I am in my bed with the blankets pulled up to my chin. Headlights are circling around the edges of my ceiling. Who is driving at this hour? Burglars, I think. Intruders, perhaps.

I turn on the lights on my way to the kitchen. I open cupboards and slam them loudly. I stomp around in my slippers, flicking lamp switches on and off, sending signals to the outside snooper, letting him know I am up and about. He will not surprise me in my bedclothes. I wrap my fur coat around me and grip the knife I keep in the right pocket precisely for this purpose. Headlights circle once more. Somewhere in the distance, an engine is humming. Then, silence. Nothing. The street is quiet. It will be hours until I hear the morning birds.

I return to my room and sit on the bed. I look out of my window and see the lights at the oil refinery pulsing. Little orange cinders across the bay at Kurnell. It looks like a birthday cake with many tiered candles – those long, thin towers that rise at different lengths and their soft, twinkling lights. The sky above it is always an odd purple, especially at night.

I am still catching my breath when I hear it: the green telephone on the nightstand. I stare at it for a while to make sure. Yes, it is ringing. When I pick up the receiver, it is cold against my ear. Static. There is no one there. Not the brisk, idiotic sound of the operator. Nothing. I wrap the spiral cord around my fingers and breathe down the line.

Hello? I say, my voice sounding hoarse because of the hour. Hello?

When he finally speaks, his voice sounds warm. His accent is strangely familiar. He tells me he is calling from the other side of the world. He wants to talk about the archipelago. He asks me if I remember leaving.

No, I tell him.

Oh, he says, but there you are! Sitting on the boat that cuts across the sea in the middle of the night. Above you there are lanterns swinging, and the sailors are singing, and you are sitting beside your sister and your mother on her battered trunk.

Turn around, he says. Look back at your island one last time.

I try to turn, but my island is no longer visible.

The man on the telephone tells me he will call again. I tell him about my trouble sleeping. How I watch the clock and am woken by the slightest noise.

You will sleep, he promises.

I lie back on the bed.

Little waves of sleep, half dreaming, until the light begins to change, and I hear the seagulls crying, and the bell on the boat is clanging, and the ravens in my backyard are cawing, and my neighbour is yelling at her dog. It is morning. It is night. I am in my bed. I am sitting on my mother's trunk. A sailor calls out: Land!

I have reached the port of the city with no memory.

2

Are you there?

Yes.

Can you hear me?

Yes.

Tell me about your island.

I don't remember.

Nothing?

It's too far.

Can't you see the shape of it? Her two peaks?

No.

Don't you remember the beach below the square?

No.

The large boulders coming out of the sea?

No.

The grotto?

No.

The sea?

All seas look the same.

Concentrate. Try to calm your mind. Don't you hear the seagulls?

Yes. But there are gulls here, too . . .

What else can you hear?

Something.

What is it? Tell me.

The rocks being dragged in and out with the tide.

What does it sound like?

Heavy. Like torrential rain, or billiard balls cascading.

The pumice cliffs, can you see them?

Yes.

Where are they?

Over there.

What do they look like?

Big white curtains.

What do they make you think of?

Money!

What do you smell? Fish guts?

No.

Where are you?

On the black-rock beach.

Tell me exactly where you're standing.

I'm in the alleyways above the dock. It's night. There's movement inside the houses, but no one is outside.

What are you doing there?

Looking through windows, waving. Knocking on the door.

They won't come?

They can't hear me.

What can you smell?

Smoke.

Smoke?

From the fumigation.

Where?

Above me. All over the island. They're trying to kill the pest on the vines.

Walk up. Try to find them.

The smoke is thick. I can't see the mountains above me.

Tell me where you are.

I'm in the square near the church. I can't go any further.

Why not?

The path stops. I can't remember the way.

You're stuck?

I can't see beyond the square. Everything is dark. There's nothing. The path stops.

Just keep walking.

I can't. It's as if there's a wall in front of me.

There's no wall.

The path stops. There's nothing. I can only remember up to the square.

Push through. Above the square is the forest, remember?

There's no forest. There's nothing.

Do you hear that?

I can't even lift my foot. There's nothing beyond the square, no forest, nothing.

The barking?

What?

Can you hear it?

Yes.

It's time to get up.

I can't.

Wake up.

I don't want to.

3

Giovanna, you remember the boat to the mainland. You remember your arrival at the port. Now, go back. Even further. Go back to when the vineyards on your island were turning white. How did it happen? How did they find the cause? Didn't they think it was the soil or the too-strong sun? The lack of rain? What about the bees? Something to do with pollination? Some kind of ferocious weed? In that first year, weren't there all kinds of theories about what, exactly, was causing your vines to die?

You all turned on the prisoners, isn't that so? You turned on them in the winter, after the nobleman left. Climbed the mountain with your rocks and shovels. And the following year, after the prisoners had been moved to another island, and the vines shot up and withered once more, who did everyone then blame? How many vineyards were lost before the idea of sabotage was abandoned?

Wasn't there talk of animals – eagles, mice, rabbits – until the men from your village went out one morning, all worked up from drinking the evening before, and shot every last rabbit they found? Wasn't there an abundance of rabbit to eat for the weeks that followed? Weren't you all gorging on rabbit, stuffing yourself with stew, so that you thought you would be happy never to taste one again?

Didn't the priest get involved? What about his anointing of the vines? Did it do anything? Don't you see him now, in the square, calming the waves of accusations between neighbours with his gentle hands?

Didn't you use poison? Weren't there other dubious methods? What was it that you put in the soil and sprinkled over the leaves? Urine of cow. Cayenne pepper. Powdered sulphur. Salt of copper. Petroleum. Coal tar. Carbon bisulphite.

How many failed harvests passed before the shipmaster received word that there was no way to kill the aphid that had been turning your vineyards white? Two? Three? Four? How quickly did his wealth dwindle once he could no longer fill his barrels with your famous wine?

Didn't he send his sons away to different continents, one by one, the eldest leaving first with the baker's daughter? Don't you see them now, waving from the ship? Didn't the baker and his family follow soon after? And did you really not suspect – even for a moment – that the shipmaster would eventually abandon you, too? Was anyone at the port when he left, stealthily, as if going on a trip? Didn't you know already that he had packed most of his possessions and sent them ahead? And wasn't it thrilling, for just a moment, when he left, and you and Giulia smashed the windows of his house with a rock and went walking through those empty rooms with a lantern, came upon the empty glass cabinets in the parlour room and, in the cobwebbed corner of the cellar, found that dusty barrel of wine, surely the last? Drunk, weren't you, in the shipmaster's house! Waltzing around the different rooms. A very sad waltz, was it not? Because all of the surrounding vineyards in the valley were dead by then, just remnants, really, all chalky white. Very eerie, like graveyards, those dead vines.

And during that bleak winter that followed, when storms cut the island off, and the fishermen couldn't take out their boats, what did you eat? How were you living? What was it like? Where are the images? Look.

Can't you see him? The man who arrived on your island long after most of the inhabitants had left? You can't remember? You don't recall? Fine. Close your eyes. Hold the telephone close to your ear. Giovanna, listen to me. I will tell you.

4

After the vineyards had withered and turned white several harvests in a row – never in the spring, always in the summer right before the grapes would usually swell – a new visitor arrived on the island. Do you remember him, Giovanna? Not the nobleman. This man came many years after. He had a thin moustache and a circular monocle that enlarged his left eye. He introduced himself as a representative of a foreign shipping company, and he brought with him many bags made from turtle skin. He conducted his business in the baker's shop, kept his files on the dusty shelves. This man had an affinity for sweets. He carried with him at all times a small tin containing cinnamon sticks – an exotic treat. Sometimes he sucked on the ends while conversing. Often, he lamented the loss of your wine.

He spoke lovingly of the nectar taste that went straight to the head. Holding his thumb and finger out in measurement, he would often say: *What I would give for one small glass.*

He noticed the empty barrels, rotting from years of winter rain and seawater, all stacked up at the port. He took a solitary walk around the island as soon as he arrived and witnessed for himself the skeletal remnants of the vineyards. The soil coated with ash. The white stems. He said it made him shiver. And you told him: *Don't walk there alone. There is bad energy*, you said.

You were sixteen when the man with the turtle bags arrived. Most of the other families from your village had left. The square was devoid of its once-rumbustious bustle. There was no longer any excitement to be had in the square.

And what did you do in those years? Walked around in circles. Went in and out of your neighbours' empty houses looking for things they might have left behind. A rusted pot, a broken chair, a chipped lamp.

Even the priest had left. The doors of the church remained open in case anyone wanted to pray. Inside, it always sounded as if someone was wailing. The wind whooshed through the building and caused the heavy doors to thud against the walls. Without the priest, the church had fallen into disarray. The yellow paint was peeling on the outside and two of the windows had been smashed. The floor was covered in a sticky layer of sand and dirt. When you went into the priest's living quarters, you found his straw mattress, some empty bottles – that was all. With no one ringing the bells, your sense of time became distorted. Days, months ate into each other. Years somehow passed.

Those of you left in the village no longer really spoke to one another. You took to grimacing whenever you came across each other unexpectedly at the fishing dock or on the beach. There was not much to talk about, except for how bad things had become and how much worse they could get.

It was not a surprise that the arrival of the man with the turtle bags roused everyone, including your mother. She took to standing outside the baker's shop with her hands pressed against the glass, eavesdropping on his meetings with the other inhabitants.

You had your suspicions about that man, it is true. You thought he might be a swindler. But you were grateful for the excitement his presence generated on the island. It was a much-needed reprieve from the monotony of your despair. Despair had become repetitive. Despair was boring. You could hardly handle waking up another morning in despair. Here was someone from the outside, where – he told you – things were different.

From his turtle bags, he retrieved photographs, charts, timetables, maps, large illustrations, an arithmometer to calculate the cost. He showed you images from other islands. Soot-stained brick buildings as large as any mountain. Wires in the sky. Metal slats on the ground. *Cities*, he said. And though you thought they were ugly, they still stirred something inside you. Besides, the man with the turtle bags was very persuasive. He showed your mother all kinds of images: overflowing vegetable carts and lively market scenes, a row of wool shops on a wide street, a bridge with carriages all loaded with sacks of wheat, factories on a wharf, abattoirs near a bay, a beach with pine trees and people picnicking on the shore – all the women holding parasols and the men ankle-deep in the water. There were images of rolling hills, grazing cows, horse cabs, happy babies, oil tankers, medicine bottles lined up in a row, advertisements painted in neat cursive on the side of a five-storey building in a language different from yours. Lakes with rowboats and harbours with ships and rivers full of golden nuggets and statues of rounded bodies and trimmed hedges and botanical gardens with gravel paths. A blue flag bearing stars.

And there was your mother, looking at the images

while the man stood opposite her sucking on his cinnamon stick. She finally asked him: *How much?* He clapped
his hands together and told her there were many options.

A ticket for the journey – he said – *blessed by the Pope himself
will guarantee entry to heaven, should any unfortunate occurrences
arise.* This was top tier. Your mother studied the ticket
and accompanying certificate, which was indeed blessed
by His Holiness – the signature surrounded by clouds
and stars. She placed it back on the counter and told
him that it did look nice. *Something cheaper?* he asked.

5

What happened after, Giovanna?

I don't know.

You left your island at night?

I can't be sure.

The wind took the scarf from your head.

I don't remember.

You saw it dancing in the sky.

If you say so.

Who was on the boat?

Mother, Giulia, me. Some of the other families from our village. Not many.

You do remember, then?

I can't see it.

You are in the boat leaving your island.

I don't think so.

Is it morning or evening?

I can't be sure.

You have blocked it out.

I can't access it.

But you arrived in Messina?

We must have.

There had been an earthquake.

Where?

In Messina.

I don't remember that.

Everything was in ruins.

6

You reach the city of M – the city without memory – and your first thought is that it reminds you of the junkyard on your island, only larger. It smells worse than the rubbish heap by the port. There is rubble on the ground and half-crumbling buildings with wires sticking out. Voices are shouting on the wharf. Everyone is selling something; none of it is of any use. Broken carriage wheels, a rowboat with holes, empty barrels. Some of them bob in the water. Sailors help your mother and Giulia out of the boat. They lift her trunk. It is late January. The wind stings your face. Your hair is matted. Your white scarf is missing. You are seventeen years old.

You are in the city of M to search for the consul. You spend your days looking for this man who cannot be found.

You are staying in the basement room of a hotel up the hill. It is on the side of the city spared from the worst of the blast. You share the room with two other families. There are no windows. You never know what time it is. You take a candle upstairs to the lobby and sometimes find it completely empty, the light outside still the blue-black of night. Other times, you come across the clerk sitting at his desk. He wears a dolman, dark red. Often, you find him crying, his chin tucked into his neck.

Every morning, you wrap your father's old jacket around you. You kneel to lace up your leather boots – the ones with the steel bottoms that once belonged to your mother. They make a clacking sound you find satisfying as you cross the city. Clack, clack, clack go your boots as you walk down the boulevard with the old theatre, which must have been grand but now looks like God has hollowed it out with a big spoon. Two walls remain standing. The rows of red chairs are covered in debris.

You reach the consul's office and find it empty. The painted wooden sign on the front door says 'Open', but when you pull it will not budge. You knock loudly, each day, to no avail. And because you do not want to return to that dank hotel room where your mother waits with Giulia, and the women from the other families often wail, and the men always snore, you walk down to the shore instead, calmed by the waves that gently lap against the wharf and the smell of the sea. Even the man urinating from the edge does not bother you.

You walk back past the fountain with the statue of King Neptune holding his trident, miraculously still intact. Scylla and Charybdis are cowering beside him with their muscular arms and squid-like legs. Perfect circular breasts – like two sets of apples. All three are surveying the sea you have crossed.

When you finally return to the hotel, your mother unfurls the official documents that must be signed. She keeps them tied with twine and nestled inside her dress. She will travel all the way to the new place like this. She says she needs to know they are there. She needs to feel them against her skin.

7

Am I saying it right?

I don't think so.

Does it sound familiar?

Not at all.

You never went to the city of M?

We must have.

You never searched for the consul?

I don't know.

The passage, how did your mother pay for it?

There was a loan system. There was a man we had to pay once we arrived here.

And the man with the turtle bags?

I have no idea what you're talking about.

But you remember the wharf, the promenade, your walks by the shore?

It has always calmed me.
What?
Being close to the sea.

8

You wake on those cold January mornings and go walking against the wind. Sea foam – large crusty bubbles – blows across the promenade. Seagulls circle above your head. Strangers around you walk with their heads down and their shoulders hunched, pulling up the collars of their jackets to shield themselves from the wind. The scene has become familiar. Everyone is trying to sell something. No one buys.

There are no ships leaving the port. You walk to the very end of the wharf where the wooden steps go down into the sea. They are moss-covered and slippery. You take the first step and squat with your hands clutching the railing. Then, you see him. The consul. Submerged in the grey-green water in his blue swimming suit with the white trimming, his arms slapping the surface. The sad clerk from the hotel was not lying when he told you that the consul is religious about his exercise, even during the winter.

An hour later you are inside his office and he is now clothed – trousers, waistcoat, white shirt, black jacket – drying his hair with a small towel. Your mother is standing nervously beside you with the documents in her hands.

Show me, he says, *quick*. His spare hand insistent. Beckoning fingers. She unties the twine herself and places the paperwork on his desk. You look around his office at the stacks of old newspapers and the hat stand with neckties and undergarments. There is an empty cage next to it with feathers at the bottom, no bird. He leans over to read the papers, lecturing your mother about the benefits of hydrotherapy, stopping to lift his head to make sure she is nodding. *A few cold laps*, he says, *will stimulate the nervous system – will keep even tuberculosis at bay.* Your mother is nodding, and Giulia is nodding, too. He leans over the documents. Little drops fall from his head. Your mother flinches beside you at the splodges on the official papers. The consul's index finger moves left to right and down the document as he reads aloud those indecipherable words. Suddenly he pauses. Taps the very bottom of the page. *I cannot sign this*, he says.

He retrieves his towel and rubs the top of his head and behind his ears, sits at his desk, takes a comb from his pocket to run through his hair. He puts the comb back and places his hands together, and that is when your mother begins to speak about the man with the turtle bags, their agreement, his promise. *Yes*, says the consul, as his finger goes up in the air and then down to the document, tapping it once more. *But look here. Do you see? He forgot the stamp.*

9

You were in the city of M.
  I don't know this part.
  In the consul's office.
  Mongrel.
  The consul?
  A smug man.
  He was talking about the stamp. Did he stamp it?
  I don't know.
  He must have. You boarded the ship.
  That's true.
  Did the ship leave from there?
  No.
  Where then?
  Naples.
  How did you get there?

I don't remember.

Do you still have the documents?

Mother kept them.

Where?

Somewhere. I . . .

You are remembering something?

Yes, something.

It's coming back?

I wouldn't say that.

Will you tell it on your own now?

No, not on my own. Not entirely, because you've told me things.

What things?

Images, places, names. You've given me these things.

Have I got it wrong so far?

I wouldn't know.

Does it ring true?

I don't think so, no. Not the facts. But the feeling of it . . .

Why not tell me what really happened?

I can't.

You don't like that version?

I can't reach it.

You can.

It's not for now.

So, what will you do then? Invent?

I'll expand on what you have already said. I'll invent from what you've given me so far. What else can I do?

Tell me, then.

10

I'm seventeen and standing at the port in Naples. The
ship we are waiting to board is called *Orient*. She is new.
Iron-hulled. Gargantuan. Bigger than any ship belonging to the shipmaster. Mother wants to know about the
route. She wants to know about the cargo. She thinks
the journey will be safer if it is transporting something
of value to its owner. There will be no barrels of wine
on board. No sacks of pumice. Mainly people, they
tell us, all travelling to the new place. And livestock to
feed the passengers on the long trip. Fifty sheep, twenty
pigs, two hundred ducks, five hundred chickens. Cows
for milking. We will be at sea for six to eight weeks.
Orient will pass through the Suez Canal, heading
south, passing the Nile to the west and the Dead Sea to
the east.

At the port, foreign sailors are shovelling coal into the bunker from the pile beside the ship. They use shovels, carts on wheels, and their hands to lob the coal into the bottom where it is fed into the boiler.

A crowd of people at the port, all anxious in their woollen jumpers and heavy jackets. It is late February. The sea a dull grey. As we make our way on board the mood – which had been one of anxious excitement, with accordions playing and people singing – suddenly turns. The other passengers are mostly men, but it is the women who push past Mother. It is the women who step on Giulia's toes. It is a woman who grabs the back of my neck and yanks it sideways as she rushes past to get the most advantageous spot on deck. Later, I watch her waving and crying, placing that violent hand of hers to her coat pocket to retrieve her white handkerchief and delicately dab her eyes.

We had no one to wave to at the port, but I still wanted to wave. I felt I had been cheated out of it by the woman who yanked my neck. On the deck, there were people surrounding us. Mother, Giulia and me. Three small bodies. Above us, beards and moustaches. The machinery rumbling somewhere beneath our feet. For some time, I did not realise that we were moving.

What would I have seen if I had prodded my way to

the back of the ship like the neck-puller? The long road that led to the port. The Pompeian red buildings and the green hills behind them. To the left, the castle, and to the right, Vesuvius – larger than our mountain.

I did not see any of it. Not one bit. I was sardined between our countrymen, all of their arms raised, jackets taken off hastily, whipping me and Mother in the face. One of them was so excited that he bent down to scoop up Giulia – now fifteen, hardly a child – and twirled her above his head. She was smiling. She got to wave to the people. Later, she told me he had hurt her armpits.

A bell rang. The port must have disappeared from view. Only then did the crowd dissipate. Only then did the woman leave her prized spot. There was nothing but water around us. The dull winter light reflecting the grey of the sea. A lull in the air. I was hungry.

The first thing I noticed when we entered the dining room was the large portrait of a foreign queen. The queen to which the *Orient* belonged. She wore a white veil on her head and a black dress with white scalloped sleeves. A blue sash. She had no neck. And those hands – ginormous. Never had I seen anyone so well fed. So why did she look so grumpy?

Because her portrait was on the wall, I imagined that

she was somewhere on the ship. When we sat down to eat, when we walked through the corridors, I kept expecting to bump into her.

11

After the long goodbyes at the port, after the handker-
chiefs have been returned to kindly sailors, after the
thrill of being at sea has settled into a methodical hum,
it becomes apparent, quite suddenly, that there are
foreign passengers on board. In the dining room, we sit
according to our group.

On the third evening we are told there will be a show.
We are asked if we have any talents. Among our group
we count twelve accordion players, a trio of harmonis-
ers, a man who is willing to hold a lit flame underneath
his finger for five minutes, an amateur soprano and a
spirited woman who performs – both on demand and
without warning – a boisterous tarantella. She need not
even hear the music to begin. She says she can summon
it in her head. On various nights throughout the

journey she will rise from her chair while some of us are still eating. She is her own accompanist and she hums madly as she moves. Spits saliva out like a wild dog. In the beginning, we are embarrassed. But as the weeks go by and we begin to see how the other group views us and learn of their discomfort at such displays, we will encourage her. Stamp our feet on the floor. Our tables will erupt in cheers whenever she rises spontaneously from her chair and makes her way to the centre of the room. We will watch her and watch the group on the other side of the room as they pretend not to notice, as they continue with their conversations, all of us picking up our plates and glasses quickly whenever the ship rocks.

Every evening, they sing their anthem to their queen. Off-key and gruff, hardly a song at all. It is the only thing that inspires any feeling in them. They like to drink. We notice this. They drink like the drunks on our island did, only they become loving to one another and then, quite unexpectedly, violent. On those nights, before the mood turns, they might walk across the room and sit beside us. They might even invite one of us to dance. There is music after dinner and one of the men from the other group has taken a liking to Giulia. He boarded at Gibraltar and is making the voyage to the new place alone. Mother thinks he must be looking for a wife. *Why doesn't he want you?* she asks.

Each night, he enters the dining room and looks for little Giulia. She waits for him to approach our table, knowing that he will do so only after consuming as much brandy or port as possible. He becomes jovial then. He is quite flattering, this older man who is sweet on Giulia. He becomes a different person than the one who entered the room. I want to ask Mother why she is permitting Giulia to dance with this older man, quite clearly a drunk. The subject is too sensitive. She is already stressed about the voyage. I do not want to rattle her.

When we pass this man in the mornings on deck he walks with his head down. He barely speaks to us. After a few glasses in the evenings, though, his mouth becomes loose. He says all kinds of things to Giulia, with Mother and me in earshot, too. Sometimes, I chaperone their laps around the deck. I linger behind and listen to him telling her that he loves her. His affection knows no bounds. Twice he has taken my arm in his. Twice he has mistaken me for Giulia. He is twelve years older than me and I see right through him. *Poor you*, I say to Giulia, and she replies that I have always been jealous.

Privately, with Mother, I begin to wonder aloud

about him and his people. About what the people in the new place will be like. These are thoughts I can express only after Mother herself has had something small to drink. A glass of sherry. A nip of port. One night, in the cabin while Giulia sleeps, Mother tells me that it would not be so bad if Giulia or I were to find a husband. *Once we are in the new place*, she says, *there won't be many people who can help us.*

Faces appear before me. I am looking at the men on board. I see their toothy grins and their bloodshot eyes. They thrust a limp hand in my face and demand that I dance with them. When I shake my head, they ask: *What's wrong with you?*

12

Operator? Yes, hello. I want to place a call.

  Number, please.

  Three four nine one two five.

  Hold the line.

  . . .

  It's connected.

  Hello?

  Hello, Giulia?

  Yes?

  It's me.

  What?

  It's Giovanna.

  What time is it?

  It's late.

  What's happened?

Nothing, just –

Giovanna, you can't call me at this hour –

I just –

What is it?

On the ship –

What?

The ship.

What ship?

That man. Do you remember? The one with the gap in his front teeth?

What?

The gap, on the deck in the evenings, the two of you –

What are you laughing at? You sound like a maniac.

Giulia, he said all those things!

. . .

Giulia?

Yes, I'm here. What time is it?

It's four –

And you want to talk now?

Yes.

. . .

Giulia, can you hear me?

Yes. I'm here.

Oh.

What do you want?

That man. What was his name? I wanted to know if you remembered it.

Who?

The man on the ship. The one from Gibraltar.

I don't know what you're talking about.

Giulia, there is this professor who calls me –

Who?

And he says that –

A professor?

Yes.

Giovanna, don't talk to him.

Why?

You don't know what he will write.

But he tells me things –

You can't trust him.

How do you know?

Because I wrote to him and then he called me and told me all kinds of lies.

Oh.

He is a liar.

What did he say?

Mother wouldn't like it.

Like what?

Us speaking to him.

Oh.

. . .

Giovanna?

Yes?

What does he want from you?

He wants to know how we came here. On the ship –

Why?

He is trying to piece together the trip. He says he is
tracing a line from the archipelago to here –

But why?

I don't know. It's for his study. He's going to write a
book and sometimes he reads me things –

What things?

The nobleman that came. He reads parts of his jour-
nal. He does this funny voice.

. . .

Giulia?

What?

Are you there?

Yes.

Oh. I couldn't hear you.

. . .

Giovanna?

Yes?

Has he said anything about me? Did he say anything

about Mother and the shipmaster? About me . . . How he thinks that Father . . .

No. Wait, what do you mean?

. . .

Giulia? Can you hear me?

Yes.

Let's talk. I want to talk.

I can't.

Giulia, talk to me.

Not now, I'm going to bed.

13

Giovanna, are you there?

Yes.

Can you hear me?

Yes.

Tell me more about the ship. Tell me about the cabin. Did it have electric lights? A latrine? Three small towels?

No. It wasn't like that. Not at all. We all slept in a large room near the machinery. There were no windows, and the straw beds were infested with mice.

You didn't promenade on the deck in your best outfits?

No one changed their clothes, not for weeks at a time. There was no privacy. Six weeks in the same under-garments. There was one public toilet on deck. People were scared to go. Everyone got sick.

What about the talent show? You said –

There were bowls full of vomit. The constant smell of that or else chloride of lime.

What did you eat?

Nothing of substance.

There was no dining hall?

Little children were sick, too.

What about Giulia's man from Gibraltar?

There was a man . . . He used to sit on one side of the room and stare at her.

From the other group?

We were all mixed together. Down there, below deck, the room was sweaty. We could smell the smoke from the boiler.

Why tell it otherwise?

I don't know.

You don't want to remember?

It's gone.

Where has it gone?

It's in the ether. Maybe I left it on the ship.

But you remember it? You remember parts of being on the ship?

Parts, yes. But things slip away.

What do you mean?

It happens all the time. Things slip away. It doesn't

have anything to do with age. One day you can call upon something and the next day it's gone.

You have always had trouble remembering?

I have had trouble holding on to certain things.

Even when you were young?

Even when I was young.

Bad things?

No, not just bad things. It's not as simple as that.

What things, then?

All kinds of things. I used to close my eyes when I had trouble remembering a word. I would concentrate on the world of the thing. I would say: *Come, thing, come.* I would try to make the conditions right for remembering. Then, somewhere down the line, it became images, not just words. I would try to trace my way back. When we first spoke, I found I could get to alleyways where we lived. I could walk around them. It was your voice that helped me up the hill. I could get to the square. I could see all of this and then nothing. Do you remember? It went black. I couldn't walk any further. I hit a wall. I couldn't get beyond. But you spoke to me. You showed me things. These conversations with you, I don't know how to say it . . . they created something new.

But where does this new version come from?

I take from things. I take any images I can. Any

sounds, feelings, dreams. I take all of it and it gets mixed up together.

And what do they make? All of these things together?

Something that feels real to me, even if it isn't. Something both here and not here. Sometimes it appears so close, I could reach out my hand and touch it.

14

Sometimes we see the curve of a coastline. Red cliffs. Sandy hills with dotted green shrubbery, like leopard spots. Tiny islands appear in the middle of the sea. Nothing on them but birds. It is the beginning of our voyage. We have been sailing for two weeks. I have taken to promenading around the deck by myself. I like the feeling of the wind on my face. I like watching the ripples fan out from the stern. Sometimes I am cautioned by one of the ship's staff. *Where is your chaperone?* they ask.

Giulia is with the man who boarded at Gibraltar. Mother is playing cards in the dining hall with the women from our group. They have nothing of value, so they gamble matchsticks. Sometimes I sit with her while she plays. She is cheerful while she is winning

– embraces me, throws her hands in the air – but when she loses, her body becomes stiff. Her back hunches. Her body folds into itself. She cannot be consoled and she will not leave the room.

I promenade on deck. Where else would I want to be?

It's on one of these walks that I see him. The ship-master. He is standing at the helm with his back to me. I know that it is him from his posture, his purple scarf, the gold on the handle of his cane. I cannot run towards him, I will be stopped by the staff if I do, and so I walk briskly, lifting the hem of my dress. I am taking long strides. My shoes are practically sliding across the floor. My hair is coming loose. He begins to move. He is weaving through the crowd at his own leisurely pace. Just as I reach him, he slips inside a door. The windows are tinted. There is a sign painted on the glass. Curved letters in green. I can't read it. I reach out for the handle, but one of the staff stops me. He says something I don't understand. He points at my dress. I think he must be saying that I am not dressed well enough. I search for the stain or rip that has caught his attention, but he laughs and shakes his head. He mimes wearing a dress himself, then waggles his index fingers from side to side right in my face. He points again to the sign on the door and folds his arms. A man from our group is passing by. *It's the smoking room*, he says. *Men only.*

I hang around outside the tinted windows. I have the urge to press my face against the glass. But both men are watching me and I am embarrassed. I walk around the deck. I do this until the sun sets. When I finally pass while the door is open, all I see are figures sitting together at circular tables – their faces obscured by all that smoke. I search for signs of him, the gold of his cane, but the door shuts. I won't see him again for the rest of the trip.

15

Port Said. The entrance of the Suez Canal. I wanted a good spot this time. I wanted to be standing at the front of the ship when we moored. I wanted to be weeping in a long white dress with a bodice and lace sleeves, holding on to my hat. It did not matter that no one would be waving back to me at the port. I had an image in my head and I wanted to play it out. I woke Mother and Giulia by clapping loudly in their faces. I told them there was no time to waste. They would not move. It was warm. Giulia barely opened her eyes. Mother's mouth was lopsided from the demons of her sleep. I grabbed her hat. What was I thinking? Only that I wanted to be the first at the front of the ship, and I was.

The deck was almost empty, only a few passengers idling around. I wanted my dress to be blowing but there was no wind, not even a flutter. The heat was immense. I was sweating. Mother's hat fitted awkwardly on my head. It sat halfway down my face. My hair underneath was damp. I wiped the back of my neck with my hand. I had no handkerchief to wave.

Land came into view. It was completely flat. Rows of palm trees and rectangular buildings and squat houses in neat, gridded lines. Several large ships, moored and silent. It was late in the afternoon. Everyone was still napping. The sun was blinding. The horn sounded, and then the bell. We were called to the dining room, where they explained: those of us who wanted to disembark had to pick up our identity cards. These instructions were only for our group. The other group could leave freely. Mother and Giulia did not want to go. Mother said she had a dream where the ship had left without us. I went to retrieve my identity card alone. *Not without an escort*, they said.

I wanted to walk around the town. Who knows what I would have seen? Instead, I watched from the ship. Watched as an elderly woman from the other group was lowered down to the port in a large, cushioned chair with her dogs on her lap, four sailors squatting beneath the chair as they walked her down. All the while she was fanning herself, tapping one of them on the head when he missed a step. She was lifted out of the chair by her escorts and off they went – I found out later – to the International Hotel.

The International Hotel had a terrace high up from which they could view the port. There were ferns in big gold pots and waiters wearing tuxedos and white gloves. Large birds that spoke from their cages. Tea was served on silver trays that were wheeled around by the staff. Electric fans whirred while the guests drank cucumber water with ice and lemon. The woman in the chair tossed her scraps on the floor and watched, with pleasure, as her dogs ate them up.

Meanwhile, I was stuck on the ship, sullen and stir-crazy. I wanted to be at the International Hotel. Instead, I listened to sounds from the streets below. I watched the sailors load the coal. They formed a long line and passed the baskets between them, singing and grunting as the sun beat down. Their skin was already inflamed. They looked like carrots wearing white uniforms. And they stayed there all night, loading coal even after the other passengers had returned from the hotel showing everyone the trinkets they had bought. Red silk slippers and notebooks bearing the image of a camel. Tins of tobacco.

I took the opportunity, after dinner, to promenade alone on deck. No one was there to tell me I couldn't. The sailors were still shovelling coal into the boiler or else they were on the wooden wharf smoking and looking up at the stars. Some of them walked down those wide streets passing a bottle between them. Music floated up to the ship from below – loose drums, horns, an oboe. It was not a waltzing song and yet I waltzed myself around the deck.

16

Passing through the Suez Canal we saw mountains on either side of the ship. At night, they were deep blue or black, but when the sun hit them in the morning they looked purple with crevasses of deep red. It depended on the light. Sometimes they were the colour of sand. It felt nice to glide past them slowly. I watched from the windows of the dining room while the women around me fanned their faces non-stop and the men took themselves to their sweaty cabins to lie down in the nude. Giulia and I took turns putting drops of water down Mother's back until one night she said she could no longer stand it and gathered up all the bedding, took us out to the deck. We were surprised to find the other passengers already there, sleeping on the floor with their limbs splayed out. It was near midnight. The stars were very close. The sky was cloudless. The heat pressed down. There was a moment when it dropped. We all felt it. In the hours before sunrise, the heat suddenly disappeared and we wrapped our linens around us and stumbled back to our cabins. We were edging closer to the equator, the sailors told us. That was why the sun shot up into the sky so fast.

I had met a girl on board of about my age. She was travelling with her sister. Most of her family were already in the new place. Each day, in the dining room, she sat alone scribbling in her diary. She wrote with her head down, forehead creased, this look of extreme concentration on her face, and then she would look up to check if we were watching. Sometimes she sat with her elbows on the table, chin resting in her palms, staring out of the window silently, until she made a little sound of triumph and then returned to her page. Watching her, I felt – I still feel – that it was horribly obnoxious. Was I jealous of her autonomy? Of the bravado she had in announcing to the rest of us in this way that she was documenting our experience? I only know that it irked me. She told me of her plan to send the diary home and have it published in the local newspaper.

I confided in Giulia, but she was not bothered. Giulia was always with her lapdog, the man from Gibraltar.

My chaperoning had become quite lax. Sometimes I watched them from the other end of the deck while they held hands, him bending down – he was quite lanky – to whisper something in her ear. I could not stand the sight of this either. I turned my attention to the churning current below me, to the other ships that passed.

When we left the Suez Canal, the sea became wide once more.

There would be another stop, they told us. Another occasion for souvenirs, this time in Colombo. Again, the other group disembarked freely without the need of their identity cards. This time, I could not watch from deck. I was too jealous.

Then it was all ocean. Monotonous blue. No land in sight. The perpetual rocking of the ship. It felt as if the waves were in your throat, threatening to come out. A man leaning overboard, a preacher from the other group, looked as though he might fall in. He looked as if he planned to, but, no, he was just sick. I watched him vomit over the railing.

17

Do you remember your arrival in the new place?

Yes, they rang the bell early. Everyone ran out on deck.

What did it look like?

Flat. No mountains. Curved bays. At the port, there were horse cabs, and everyone was yelling. A bright room for medical examinations.

And then?

And then there were other rooms. So many different rooms belonging to people we did not know. In the morning, the sound of a cockatoo screeching – like a child being strangled.

The squawking?

We didn't know what it was.

What else was different?

Everything. The smells, the sounds, the people. Even the sky.

And?

And then it became normal. And the archipelago became the foreign thing.

You never returned?

We never left here again. Mother said if she had known how far it really was, she wouldn't have got on the ship.

And you?

I became a different person. A shy person. I smiled a lot when I talked to strangers. I searched crowds for friendly-looking faces. I spoke in a shy, non-threatening way.

Why?

I was scared. I became a scared person.

What were you afraid of?

Everything. I barely spoke. Every interaction was difficult. Every interaction had to be judged. Is this person angry at me? Do they understand me? Why are they making that face? Are they dangerous? Actually, I rarely thought of danger. I just wanted to be liked. I was ecstatic if someone was nice to me. In those days, if someone were to smile at me in the street, I would have followed them anywhere.

But you were scared?

It's difficult to explain. I had nothing solid to hold onto. I had nothing concrete to show of myself. I no longer knew who I was because I no longer had the words to express it. I felt like a walking void. I could not communicate.

You had trouble with the language.

I longed to speak. But I couldn't, so I retreated into myself.

And Giulia?

Giulia was the baby. She glided along. She liked the new place. She picked up the language easily.

And your mother?

Mother spoke about nothing but our island. She created a different island in her mind. She cried constantly over our departure. She missed her people. That's why she joined the association.

What association?

For the archipelago. It was a society. A kind of club for people from the islands and the mainland, too. There were sailors from the archipelago who were now living in Ulladulla, Wollongong, Woolloomooloo.

You met them?

Yes.

Where?

At the ball.

There was a ball?

Yes.

This really happened?

Yes.

18

Late spring, Mother, Giulia and I took the newly electric tram from La Perouse all the way into the city. It was mahogany with cream trimmings. We passed the thermal power station and the racecourse, and I rang the bell for the Centennial Park stop, where we walked across the dewy grass with bats circling above our heads. It was early evening. Hours before, Mother had sat on the bed at our lodgings and said she no longer wanted to go. She was nervous. We helped her into her woollen skirt and silk blouse and did up all the buttons at the back. By then, we had been living here for three years. Giulia was eighteen and already had a new beau.

The ball was held in the Paddington Town Hall and the building had been dressed for the occasion. A giant bow adorned the archway at the front door. There was even a sign welcoming us – those of us from the archipelago and the mainland, too. This was before the wars, before the internment camps, before the association was officially disbanded.

Inside, a banquet had been set up and there were trestle tables with lace tablecloths and flower arrangements. At one point, confetti fell from the ceiling while the band on stage played songs Mother recognised and she was wiggling in her chair. The founders of the association – all men – sauntered around patting heads and pinching cheeks. Giulia's beau, originally from the mainland, arrived and they danced around the room. Whenever they passed, I saw Mother's hands tighten into little fists, saw her stick out her leg like she meant to trip them. She did not like him. *Too short*, Mother said. *Flabby. Nose like a pig.* But when they finished the waltz and came to sit with us, Mother reached out both hands and the beau took them in his and she was saying to him: *My son.*

By the end of the evening, the founders of the association were near drunk and even Mother was brimming with wine. Little wooden boxes lined with purple velvet were passed around the room and the founders went up on stage to ask for donations. Earlier, they had spoken of the work they had done for the community and, it was true, we had only found our lodgings because of them. Mother was generous. She pulled out her pouch and fed her coins into the slot.

The mood changed. It happened quickly. I can still remember it. If I close my eyes, I am there.

The music tapers off. Accordion notes are left hanging in the air. The founders announce the largest donations. They say they are proud to introduce a new benefactor and ask him to walk into the centre of the empty dance floor. And when they call out his name, I feel my throat close. Even Mother, in her inebriated state, recognises it. We look into the crowd of men in their suits and bow ties and we watch him, as if in slow motion, walk into the middle of the room. It is the shipmaster's second-eldest son. Recently arrived in the country from America.

Mother wants to leave. She is overcome with emotion. Giulia and I walk her out the door and down to the street and we hear the muffled sound of the band beginning to play again. Outside, a tram rushes past. It is night. There is a strong breeze and the three of us are shivering. From out of the dark a drunk approaches us. *Ladies*, he is saying, *ladies*. We see a tram stopping and rush to get on it. The conductor comes and I take out

Mother's pouch to buy the ticket, only she has no coins left. It's not even our route. Giulia explains this to the conductor and he takes pity on us. I feel such kindness towards him that I want to kiss his lumpy face.

We sit on the brown leather seats. Mother beside me and Giulia on the one opposite. As we move, I can make out the gate of the park, but we are on the opposite side, travelling up some unknown hill, the carriage jolting from side to side. When we reach the top, I see the black harbour below and the brick factories and large warehouses on the shore lit by the moon. The tram begins to make its way down the hill, gathering speed; the carriage is shaking and the light inside the cabin is pulsing. The window is open and the wind is fresh on our faces. Mother is resting her head on my arm with her eyes closed and Giulia is staring silently out of the window, not saying a word. I am looking for something – any landmark – that I recognise so that we can get off. The carriage jolts and Mother lifts her head, looks out the window at the empty street, pitch dark, and says in a voice that sounds small, like a child's, *Giovanna, where are we?*

19

It's late.

Yes.

You can't sleep?

No.

What do you do to pass the time?

Look out my window. Listen for you.

To keep you company?

Yes.

Do you want to talk about it?

No.

You never saw your island again?

Never.

But recently . . . on the television?

Yes, but –

You saw a programme about the archipelago.

It was unrecognisable.

What did you see?

A silly film to promote our island. It looked so different. It had been rebuilt. There were vineyards growing
again and they were making wine, but the square was
filled with shops, little boutique shops selling identical
hats. Holiday hats! And then all those bodies, half nude,
all those pink and red bodies – it was in colour, of course
– burnt from the sun and walking into the stores to buy
those stupid hats. There were roads and cars and I saw
a couple embrace at the top of our mountain. They
were kissing as the sun went down and I felt ill at the
very sight of it. There were images of the other islands
and they spoke of ours as the greenest. They talked
of her in terms of green. They said nothing about the
shipmaster, nothing about the men. They mentioned
the phylloxera. They said it no longer mattered.

It was unrecognisable to you?

I felt I was watching another island. It was evening
and all the lights in the house were off and the television
was beaming these images to me in the dark. These
bright, colourful images, and a voice was speaking –
British, enunciated, annoying – about my island as a
holiday destination. I wanted to erase those images, but
I couldn't. Some kind of replacement took place without

my permission. Watching the programme replaced my own images of the island.

And now?

And now ... when I close my eyes, I can no longer walk up to the square. All I see are those half-naked bodies on the black-rock beach.

Would you like to go back?

I don't think so ...

You are happy here?

It is all that I know.

This is your island?

Not at all.

20

I will remember one last thing for you.

A sailor dressed in drag. Red lipstick smeared. The head of a mop as his wig. The captain's first assistant parading as King Neptune. Streamers and tendrils, his face painted blue. That costume, where did they get it? It was tatty. It had been overused. It was what they brought out each time the ship crossed the equator. A ritual. We all stood on deck to watch the ceremony. I found myself locking eyes with the girl writing her diary of the trip. She was already writing the scene in her head.

When we crossed, it was the middle of the day. We were far from land. The blue of the water and the blue of the sky met on the horizon, where the colour smudged. That line – it appeared to be fizzling. And I saw it. Our island among the others in the archipelago. I knew it was ours from the two peaks. It made perfect sense to me. We had crossed from north to south. We had crossed over into something else. At the time, I imagined that everything on this side of the equator would be the same as the other, only upside down. That this half of the world would mirror the other. I saw our island and thought it completely normal. I told no one at the time.

Years later, I sought out a woman who knew about such things, and I told her: I saw our island. I saw the archipelago as we were passing the equator and the sailors around me were dancing and singing and praying, paying their respects to King Neptune. They were asking to be brought back safely. And this woman – who had such expertise – said that the islands had not been there at all. That this was a mistake people often made at sea. That it was only the light on the horizon that made it appear as though there were things there. And she told me the name. *Fata Morgana*, she said. A superior mirage.

And so, even now, when I look for things that are no longer there, or when I am spooked, when a memory or a fallacy or a fiction appears unexpectedly, I think to myself: *Fata Morgana, Fata Morgana.*

AUTHOR'S NOTE

In the late nineteenth century, two unrelated events occurred on the Aeolian Islands of Sicily – Lipari was decreed a place of habitual detention and the phylloxera epidemic, which had been spreading through Europe, finally reached Salina, prompting economic collapse and mass migration. One visitor to the archipelago during this period was the Archduke Ludwig Salvator of Austria. I have drawn loosely from his life and work. A novel has many origins, and not all of them are tangible. My Archduke is an imaginary figure, and the island that appears here is an imagined place.